“Are you going to Saturday’s house-raising?”

“I was invited, *ja*,” Adele answered, and gave a wistful smile. “I wouldn’t miss it. It’ll be the first house-raising I’ve been to in a long, long time.”

Isaiah wanted to ask why, but didn’t. It occurred to him how little he knew about Adele. Had she left the Amish and was just now returning? Had she moved from back east to escape something painful in her past? He simply didn’t know.

But he wanted to. Certainly her overtures of friendship to his daughter, Clara, paved the way, but Adele was a woman he wanted to know much better. However, her natural shyness and diffidence were difficult to overcome.

But she would be at the house-raising. So would most everyone else in the community. He would try to pick up as much information as he could about his beautiful coworker.

Impulsively he decided to tell a small lie. “By the way,” he said casually, “did Clara mention the dinner invitation?”

Living on a remote self-sufficient homestead in North Idaho, **Patrice Lewis** is a Christian wife, mother, author, blogger, columnist and speaker. She has practiced and written about rural subjects for almost thirty years. When she isn't writing, Patrice enjoys projects, such as animal husbandry, small-scale dairy production, gardening, food preservation and canning, and homeschooling. She and her husband have been married since 1990 and have two daughters.

Books by Patrice Lewis

Love Inspired

The Amish Newcomer
Amish Baby Lessons
Her Path to Redemption
The Amish Animal Doctor
The Mysterious Amish Nanny
Their Road to Redemption
The Amish Midwife's Bargain
The Amish Beekeeper's Dilemma
Uncovering Her Amish Past
The Amish Bride's Secret
An Amish Marriage Agreement
The Amish Baker's Redemption

Visit the Author Profile page at LoveInspired.com.

THE AMISH BAKER'S REDEMPTION

PATRICE LEWIS

If you purchased this book without a cover you should be aware that this book is stolen property. It was reported as "unsold and destroyed" to the publisher, and neither the author nor the publisher has received any payment for this "stripped book."

ISBN-13: 978-1-335-62143-6

Recycling programs for this product may not exist in your area.

The Amish Baker's Redemption

Copyright © 2026 by Patrice Lewis

All rights reserved. No part of this book may be used or reproduced in any manner whatsoever without written permission.

Without limiting the exclusive rights of any author, contributor or the publisher of this publication, any unauthorized use of this publication to train generative artificial intelligence (AI) technologies is expressly prohibited. Harlequin also exercises their rights under Article 4(3) of the Digital Single Market Directive 2019/790 and expressly reserves this publication from the text and data mining exception.

This is a work of fiction. Names, characters, places and incidents are either the product of the author's imagination or are used fictitiously. Any resemblance to actual persons, living or dead, businesses, companies, events or locales is entirely coincidental.

For questions and comments about the quality of this book, please contact us at CustomerService@Harlequin.com.

® is a trademark of Harlequin Enterprises ULC.

Love Inspired
22 Adelaide St. West, 41st Floor
Toronto, Ontario M5H 4E3, Canada
www.LoveInspired.com

HarperCollins Publishers
Macken House, 39/40 Mayor Street Upper,
Dublin 1, D01 C9W8, Ireland
www.HarperCollins.com

Printed in Lithuania

He that is without sin among you,
let him first cast a stone at her.
—*John* 8:7

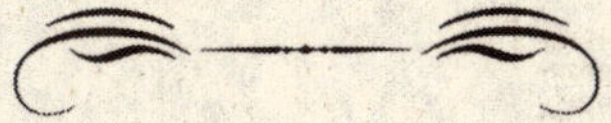

To God, for blessing me with my husband and daughters, the best family anyone could hope for.

Chapter One

Adele Bontrager added milk, water and butter to a large saucepan and started it heating over a slow flame on the industrial stove located in the store's bakery. While it warmed, she mixed flour, sugar, yeast and a bit of salt in a large bowl. She dusted a large wooden bread board with flour in preparation for the kneading.

"Dinner rolls?" inquired Mabel Yoder, the older Amish woman who co-owned Yoder's Mercantile in the tiny town of Pierce, Montana. The bakery was part of the mercantile, which made Mabel her boss.

"*Ja*," replied Adele. She paused to re-pin her *kapp*, which had a tendency to come loose during the day's work. She was still getting used to wearing it again. She washed her hands and donned latex gloves. "That restaurant in town liked the sample rolls we brought them so much, they've given us a standing order for ten dozen rolls a day."

"Ach, that's *gut* news!" Mabel smiled. "You've certainly expanded the bakery's repertoire. I'm so glad we hired you."

"Me too." Adele smiled at her employer. "Though if we get any busier, we'll need more than just me to handle the workload."

"That's what I wanted to tell you. The head baker we hired is finally on his way from Indiana."

"Oh, that's *wunnerschee*! It's been, what, at least two months since you hired him?"

"*Ja*, something like that."

"What was the delay, do you know?" She checked the temperature on the milk.

"*Nein*. I gather it was some sort of family issue, but I don't know the particulars. But he's on his way and should be here by tomorrow and will start work on Monday of next week. At last you'll have some help in the bakery."

"Or he'll have help from me. I will gladly defer to his greater experience, especially since he's had experience managing a commercial bakery back East." Adele poured the warmed milk mixture into the bowl with the dry ingredients and began stirring. "I can't tell you how much I'm enjoying this work. Baking is something I've always liked doing, but I neglected it over the past few years. Now I can do it for a living."

Mabel looked sympathetic. She was one of the few people who knew Adele's story, and Adele trusted the older woman's discretion.

"I'm so glad," Mabel replied softly. She smiled and returned to the main portion of the store.

Adele watched the plump figure disappear from sight. As owners of the store, Mabel and her husband, Abe, had given Adele a job even though she brought no experience with her, and Adele was grateful for the opportunity. She was determined to never make them regret that decision.

This job was just the first step in redeeming a lifetime of bad choices. Adele uttered a silent prayer of thanksgiving and began kneading the dough.

These last two months had been a revelation to her. Everything about the Amish lifestyle she had rejected when she was younger now seemed like a refuge. She felt like she was almost frantically embracing what she'd denied before, and almost couldn't do enough to stay on the straight and narrow path toward baptism. Since arriving in Pierce, seeking sanctuary from yet another love affair gone bad, she had followed the advice of the bishop—reinforced by her younger sister—on how to reclaim her life and her dignity. Adele had many regrets, but returning to the church was not one of them.

Now she felt at home among her fellow church members. She was making friends, she had a place to live, she had adopted a pair of kittens, she found she liked working with her hands, she was rediscovering her love of embroidery and she'd become friends with her sister and her new husband. She was—for the first time in her life—content.

Or *almost* content.

She realized she was kneading the bread dough with unnecessary vigor, and consciously made an effort to slow her movements. She had flashbacks every so often, moments of piercing clarity about those times she knew she was sinning against *Gott* but continued anyway. Her biggest regret in life was giving up her baby, Helen, for her sister to raise.

The bishop reassured her *Gott* was all about forgiveness. Now if only Adele could forgive herself.

She finished kneading the dough and covered the bowl with a clean towel, then set it in the warming oven to rise. Then she turned her attention to making turnovers, which sold extremely well in the store.

"I could use three quarts each of apple pie filling and blueberry pie filling," she called to her coworker Cara, who worked in the community cannery on the opposite side of the room.

"You got it," Cara called back. "Do you want any cherry?"

"*Nein*, just apple and blueberry. Those seem to sell the

best." Adele began rolling out sheets of puff pastry and cutting them to size.

Her pretty coworker loaded a rolling cart with the requested filling and brought it over to the bakery side of the room. Adele took a moment to admire the colorful jars. "You sure do *gut* work, Cara. I never learned to can."

"*Danke*. Remember, I can teach you the process whenever you like."

"I'd like to learn, someday. Maybe when I have a garden of my own."

In the two months since starting to work at Yoder's Mercantile, she had watched Cara and her *Englisch* assistant, Lucy, preserve hundreds of jars of food during the cannery's busy season. Now it was slower, since most of the harvest had been put up for the year, and the cannery was back to producing foodstuffs to sell in the store. This time of year, their specialty was various pie fillings, since Thanksgiving was just a couple weeks away.

With the bakery operational, the mercantile had expanded its operations and increased its popularity with customers. Settling into her new job, Adele admired Cara's and Lucy's activities and hoped that one day she, too, would be as skilled.

As it was, she was thirty-three years old and heading into the holiday season as the proverbial cat lady, with only a pair of kittens to come home to rather than a *hutband* and *kinner*. Her only child was being raised by her sister Olivia. Adele had many regrets in life, and abandoning her own baby was the biggest. But little Helen was thriving in her sister's care, and Adele knew when to leave well enough alone.

With the turnovers prepared, Adele turned her attention back to the dinner rolls and soon had them cut and shaped into the desired appearance. She set them back in the warming oven for the second rising, then popped the turnovers into one of the commercial ovens to bake. The smell, she knew, would waft throughout the store, and customers would line up for fresh turnovers.

By the time the day's work was done, Adele was left with a feeling of accomplishment. She removed the dusty outer apron she wore at the bakery, said goodbye to her coworkers and mounted the bicycle she used to get to and from work.

Pierce was a remote little town of 3,500 in the northwestern part of Montana. The Amish settlement three miles outside the city limits was nothing but a collection of homes and farms built from a huge ranch that had gone up for sale a few years before, purchased by the church and available for settlement by those escaping more crowded conditions back East.

Adele was residing in a small rental cabin deep within the boundaries. As she pedaled down the gravel road leading to her home, she enjoyed the feeling of autumn sunlight on her shoulders. She was learning to appreciate the simple joys of life now, rather than reaching for the excitement of exotic destinations and a jet-set lifestyle with a succession of men.

She glided to a stop in front of her cabin and parked her bike near the front door. Inside, her two kittens came tumbling over to greet her, and Adele squatted down to scoop them up. She hugged them, thinking how much she enjoyed their company in her quiet cabin. Would she ever come home to anything else besides felines?

She released the wiggling creatures and set about making herself some dinner, including two of the fresh turnovers she'd made that afternoon that the Yoders permitted her to take home.

She seated herself at the plain kitchen table and ate her dinner, looking around the tiny living space and thinking it needed something besides the extreme basics to make it more like a home. She'd spent the last fifteen years living among luxurious furnishings and wanted nothing to do with such trappings any longer. But this stark bareness was too much in the other direction. Though she had a tiny woodstove for warmth, she wanted at least a carpet of some sort to keep the floor warm as winter approached.

Well, she was earning money now. Her first few paychecks had gone to necessities. Maybe with her next paycheck, she could afford to add a personal touch or two to her rental cabin.

After dinner, despite the coolness of the evening, she sat on a rocking chair on the front porch and watched the kittens tumble about the yard. It was then that a dire thought struck her: She would be working with a man.

Mabel Yoder mentioned the new head baker would start work in the bakery on Monday. But after Adele's promise to both her sister and the bishop, that might be a problem.

Isaiah King finished his breakfast in grim silence. Across the table, his seventeen-year-old daughter, Phoebe, ate in similar silence. Her sulky expression marred what was otherwise a pretty face. She had been this way for at least a year, and Isaiah was unable to figure out how to deal with her.

"We'll find a farm as soon as possible," he informed her, cutting through the silence. "Then we'll have more room. Meanwhile, I'll make some inquiries about a job for you in town. It will give you something to do…" *Instead of sulking all day*, he added silently.

Phoebe shrugged but said nothing. Isaiah suppressed a

familiar feeling of irritation at his nearly grown daughter's refusal to reply.

She hadn't always been this way. Until her *Rumspringa*, she was a normal happy youngie who chattered his ear off and loved indulging in her hobby of making braided rag rugs. But then she had become involved with some *Englischer* youth, and her whole attitude had changed in the span of a few months. Now she was sullen and uncooperative, and Isaiah was at a loss for what to do.

He had responded to the call for a professional baker at this newish Amish settlement all the way across the country in hopes the move might separate Phoebe from bad influences. So far it had done the opposite: It had sent the teen deeper into broodiness.

Not for the first time, Isaiah wondered if he should have remarried after his wife had died when Phoebe was ten. It was a vulnerable time for a girl to lose her mother, and now he felt somewhat helpless to draw his beloved only child out of her teenage angst.

He sighed and uttered a prayer for Phoebe, then prepared for his first day of work.

"I'll be gone until after five o'clock," he told her and kissed her on the cheek as was his habit. "Even though this won't be our permanent home, feel free to arrange it however you like."

"*Ja, danke*," Phoebe muttered, managing to make the expression of gratitude sound ungrateful.

He used the walk to town to compose his thoughts. While he had secured the job more than two months ago, it had taken that long to sell his farm, tie up loose ends, say goodbye to family and friends…and disentangle Phoebe from the influences drawing her away from the church and toward the secular world. So far, his daughter hadn't forgiven him for that action.

The walk of three miles wasn't so bad on a late fall day. His buggy was being shipped and wouldn't arrive for another week or two. He had to purchase a horse as well. He would ask his new employers, Abe and Mabel Yoder, if there was room to stable a horse during the colder months.

And all the way into town, he fretted about Phoebe. At seventeen years old, it wasn't that she needed supervision. But he worried that somehow, in some way, even in this brand-new location, she would find some way to get into trouble.

Yoder's Mercantile was easy to find on the town's Main Street. It was a large emporium, with a broad porch with steps in front and a ramp at one end. The porch had buckets of fresh autumn blooms—mums and zinnias and black-eyed Susans—and the windows displayed a variety of goods, including quilts and soaps with a harvest theme.

Stepping inside, a quick scan revealed the store was separated into various departments, including a coffee area with seating, where *Englisch* townspeople were sipping drinks, with some working on laptops. The wooden floor beneath his feet squeaked in a pleasant fashion as he closed the door behind him. Subdued autumn decor highlighted the space. Everything was exquisitely clean and tidy. He approached the register, where an older Amish man rang up a customer's purchase.

Waiting politely until the customer had left, he spoke in German to the man. "I'm looking for Abraham Yoder."

"I'm Abe Yoder." The man eyed him and smiled. "Are you Isaiah King?"

"*Ja.*" Isaiah reached over and shook the man's hand. "It took me long enough to show up, didn't it?"

"But we're so glad you're here at last. Mabel!" he called, catching the attention of a plump older woman working in the coffee area. "Here's our new baker!"

Mabel instantly came around the counter, wiping her hand on her apron. "*Welkom, welkom*!" she exclaimed, a smile wreathing her face. "So happy to meet you!"

Isaiah was warmed by their greetings. Following a chattering Mabel, he was toured around the store and shown each of the sections.

"We're constantly expanding," Mabel explained as she paused by a display of soaps. "We have a wide selection of talent in the church community and do whatever we can to showcase it. A couple years ago, we opened the community cannery as a way to provide canned goods for the store as well as give our church members a place to preserve their fall harvests. We left room in the cannery to open an in-house bakery as well. We hired a woman a couple months ago who's been doing fine, but she has no experience in a commercial facility and says she's more than happy to be your assistant baker."

Isaiah glanced around the store. "Where is the bakery?"

"Over here." Mabel led the way toward a connecting door into the building next door, a spacious room with a bank of tall windows on the south side that lit up the facility. The room was divided along its width by a half wall, with the cannery on one side and the bakery on the other.

Mabel stopped at the cannery. "This is Cara Miller, our head canner."

"How do you do?" he asked, reaching out to shake hands with the pretty Amish matron.

"Glad to have you here," she replied, hastily wiping her hands on a towel and returning the handshake.

"And this is our bakery. Adele Bontrager, this is Isaiah King. He'll be the head baker."

Isaiah was stunned. His new coworker was the most beautiful woman he had ever seen, with chocolate-brown eyes, almost black hair, a perfect nose and high cheekbones. It was seldom he saw such physical perfection in anyone. He saw tiny laugh lines at the corners of her eyes, the only indication she was probably just a couple years younger than himself. Otherwise she could have passed for not much older than his daughter.

Yet the moment she saw him, it was almost as if she shut down. She mumbled, "Nice to meet you," then lowered her head over a bowl of dough she was mixing.

She remained silent as Mabel showed him around the facility. The equipment was a mixture of state-of-the-art and old-school, as befitted an Amish commercial facility. He had spent several years running a commercial bakery in Indiana, so it was familiar territory.

"This is our weekly schedule," Mable concluded, showing him a notebook with pages encased in plastic protectors. "It shows what outstanding orders we have from various restaurants in town, as well as what items we carry—or would like to carry—in the store. Except for the restaurant orders, the rest is variable, so if you have a specialty, by all means let me know. You might consider adding Thanksgiving- and Christmas-themed foods, for example, since customers have been asking."

"*Ja gut.*" He flipped through the pages, impressed. The Yoders were incredibly organized. "In my old bakery, I used to make a braided sweet bread in the shape of a turkey, believe it or not. It was very popular this time of year."

"Ooh, *ja.* We'd like that." Mabel pointed to the wall shared with the main store. "Eventually we want to remove this wall and give the bakery its own service area, but for now all baked goods will have to be brought into the main part of the store and sold near the coffee area where we sell pastries and other specialties. But for now, it's somewhat isolated from the store."

"I agree with you about the open concept," he said with a grin. "There's nothing better than the smell of fresh-baked bread to bring in customers."

"*Ja*, you're right," agreed Mabel, with a twinkle in her eyes. "It's one of the reasons we brought in an in-house bakery."

Isaiah realized he was in the presence of a marketing genius. Mabel and Abe Yoder had clearly started this store from the ground up, and they had both the foresight and the experience to broaden the business to encompass a wide variety of goods—including the marketing ploy of fresh-baked bread. He admired their business smarts.

Mabel left him to get familiar with the bakery's layout. Left alone with Adele, he tried to engage her in conversation, but he could barely get two words out of her. She seemed shy to the point of fearful. How could such a beautiful woman not exude confidence?

He didn't know why, but some instinct told him not to push. Instead he embarked on a leisurely tour of the bakery, examining its equipment, peering into cabinets, reviewing the recommended recipes and mentally inventorying the supplies of flour, sugar, yeast, spices and other staples.

Spying one ingredient, he addressed Adele. "Have you made any loaves of rye bread?"

"*Nein*," she whispered, her head bent over the rolls she was shaping.

"I have an excellent recipe for sourdough rye," he said.

"I'll clear with the Yoders that it will be acceptable and then get a starter going."

Adele didn't answer, so he shrugged and went to inquire of Mabel Yoder if rye bread would be an acceptable addition to the repertoire.

"*Ja*, it would!" the older woman exclaimed. "I love rye bread."

"*Gut*. I'll get some sourdough starter going then." He hesitated, then lowered his voice. "Is there something wrong with the bakery assistant? She's barely spoken a word to me. Have I offended her in some way?"

"*Nein*." Mabel spoke immediately. "Don't let her bother you. I'm not at liberty to discuss anything, but I'll only say she's had a tough past. Leave her alone. She's far more likely to come out of her shell that way."

He nodded, taking the advice seriously. "*Ja gut*, I'll do that. She certainly seems competent, though I confess it would be easier to coordinate our efforts if she would talk to me."

Mabel hesitated. "She may not want to," she admitted. "Just be gentle with her. She's a *gut* person and a hard worker. Once she feels more comfortable around you, I'm sure she'll relax."

It was then that Isaiah had a head-clunk moment. He'd heard about situations where women who had been sexually assaulted were extremely skittish around men, any man. If this was the case with Adele, he could understand both her shyness as well as Mabel's discretion. He mentally vowed to do nothing that would make her uncomfortable.

"*Danke* for telling me," he said. "I'll follow the weekly schedule and leave her to work on her own, since she obviously knows what she's doing."

It would be strange, Isaiah reflected as he made his way

back to the bakery, to both work with and not work with an assistant baker. But if Adele had some tragic misfortune in her past, he didn't want to become a monster in her eyes because he was too forward or pushy.

Besides, he had other things to think about…namely, how well his daughter would settle into her new home.

Chapter Two

Adele rode her bicycle back home after her first full day of working with the new head baker, Isaiah King. She felt exhausted out of proportion to the day's labor. It wasn't the work that had tired her; she was used to that. Instead, she felt exhausted from avoiding everything from eye contact to verbal conversation with her new colleague.

She didn't like that she was warring inside herself. A lifetime of catering to men in the most carnal sense was combatting with her newfound desire to become the upstanding Amish woman her sister, Olivia, was. She carried with her a lifetime of guilt—guilt over letting down her father, who did his best to raise his daughters after he was widowed; guilt over "using" Olivia for her own selfish purposes for years and years; and guilt over abandoning her own child, forcing Olivia to pick up the slack. Could she ever purge herself of so much sin?

She wanted to try. Her sister had laid out a roadmap for her to return to the church, later reinforced by the bishop. Her first stricture was to stay away from men. After fifteen years of doing nothing but being arm candy, Adele understood this was the best way to achieve her goal of becoming baptized. She felt very much like the woman at the well in the biblical story of redemption. She, too, felt like her past sins were so gapingly huge, forgiveness was barely possible.

Yet she knew anything was possible…if she stayed away from men.

Ironically, Isaiah was a man who seemed interesting. He had dark blond hair and kindly blue eyes, and seemed a few years older than herself. She knew he was widowed and had a teenage daughter. He was utterly unlike the men she had been with before—powerful and wealthy men who appreciated her for her looks, but who seldom bothered to learn anything about what she was like on the inside.

A year ago, she wouldn't have looked twice at someone like Isaiah. Now her life had altered, and the stability and unchanging morals he represented were far more attractive.

That, of course, guaranteed he would never be interested in her. Sure, he might be interested at first, thanks to her beautiful face—Adele was coming to view her beauty as a curse—but once he learned about her past, he would run in the other direction. She wouldn't blame him.

She collapsed into the single rocking chair inside her rental cabin, with her kittens clamoring at her feet. She hauled them onto her lap and buried her face in their soft fur. These little creatures, strays she had adopted shortly after arriving, had surely been sent by *Gott* to offer her comfort and love during a time she felt comfortless and unloved.

No, that wasn't quite true. Her sister, Olivia, had offered her comfort and love during a time she had least deserved it, and Adele was beyond grateful for her sibling's support as she embarked on this new life. And yet…the years stretched before her, lonely and bleak, as she realized she would never have the things her sister had: a farm, a *hutband*…and Adele's very own baby.

But at least she had two kittens.

Sighing, she opened the rental cabin's front door and stepped out onto the tiny porch, equipped with its own rocking chair. The sun was just about to set, and the chill autumn air—smelling faintly of wood smoke as well as the apples from a wild tree growing along the road—cleansed her mind. The kittens, freed from the confines of the cabin, darted around the lawn, batting at leaves and wrestling together. She smiled at their antics.

She remembered what her sister had told her two months ago, when she had shown up, completely destitute, desperate to make a change. Olivia had said she must learn to love herself. Adele realized that despite the physical beauty *Gott* had given her, she had never truly loved herself. She had never developed the capacity to be alone. Being alone was too frightening; it meant self-analysis, something she had avoided for as long as she could remember.

Now, living alone, she was forced into the solitude she had dreaded...and found it wasn't so dreadful after all. Yes, it gave her the opportunity to examine her sinful past; but rather surprisingly, it also gave her the opportunity to pray for forgiveness. She realized she had no skills, nothing except this new job to allow her to earn a living through something other than her looks.

She was starting over. She was a mature woman of thirty-three, yet in some ways she felt like a youngie just returning from a *Rumspringa*.

She went inside and made herself a frugal meal of lentils and rice, then went to sit in the rocking chair on the porch so she could eat her dinner in the fresh air, thinking about the day. Isaiah had politely tried to engage her in conversation in the bakery, but she found she could barely meet his eyes. For too long, men had looked at her and only seen the superficial exterior, to the point where her own inner strength had atrophied and she gave men the only thing they wanted.

But since one of the prerequisites to returning to the church was to avoid men, Adele wondered how she would handle a work environment that included Isaiah. She wanted to be independent, to stand on her own two feet. So she would be cordial to Isaiah, but not friendly. She was done with men.

The sun dropped below the mountain ridge, and Adele shivered as the air cooled. She stood up and made ready to go inside to light the lamp, when a movement caught her eye.

A young Amish woman—a teenager, really—was walking down the gravel road. She had an expression of sulkiness on her face that somehow reminded Adele of herself at that age. The youngie didn't even glance at the rental cabin, but trudged on down the road, looking like a thundercloud was hanging over her head.

Adele felt a twinge of sympathy for whatever was afflicting the girl. How often had she, at the same age, roamed restlessly? She had wanted nothing more than to leave her entire upbringing behind her. She had wanted excitement, thrills, glamor.

Well, she had gotten her wish—and lived to bitterly regret it. Now here she was, almost past her prime, with nothing to show for it except a baby being raised by her sister and a photo album depicting past exotic destinations.

The youngie continued down the road until she was lost in the gloaming. Adele shrugged and went inside. She wondered who the girl was and why she was out alone at this hour.

She called in the kittens, who seemed reluctant to leave

their games behind, so Adele went out to the yard to fetch them. "You naughty things," she scolded them gently, dropping a kiss on each furry head. "There are coyotes out at this hour. I don't want anything eating you."

She released the animals into the cabin, lit the lamp and started a fire in the small woodburning stove to heat the cabin. She tidied her mess from dinner, made tea, pulled out one of the blueberry turnovers she'd made that afternoon and sat down with an embroidery project, rocking gently in the chair.

She was rediscovering her enjoyment of needlework and brought the finished projects in to Yoder's Mercantile, where the Yoders sold them as part of their profile of Amish talent. At the moment, she was creating a fanciful scene with oak leaves and acorns. When finished, it would be sold still mounted in its hoop.

But rather than concentrating on the stitchery in front of her, she found herself surveying the rental cabin. She'd lived here for two months now, and it still had nothing but the bare-bones furnishings that came with it. The space had no curtains, no carpet, no furniture beyond the rocking chair she now occupied and a kitchen table with two chairs. The bedroom held a bed and a bedside table, and that was it. A woodburning cookstove straddled the room, keeping autumn's cold temperatures at bay.

With winter coming on, she would be indoors more and decided she needed to make things more comfortable. Payday was tomorrow. Maybe it was time to earmark some of her earnings for furnishings. She envisioned an area rug in both the tiny bedroom and this living room. She could hand sew some curtains to cover the windows. She might purchase another rocking chair in case she ever had a visitor. She might even indulge in a tablecloth for the kitchen table.

Pleased with the prospect of trimming the cabin to new standards, she scrounged up a sheet of paper and a pen and started making a list. It was the first time in her life she had a place of her own, and she looked forward to personalizing it in some way.

Olivia was an expert basketmaker, so Adele knew she could impose on her sister to provide some basic storage bins. What else could she use? A small bookcase? An end table by the rocking chair to hold the oil lamp? A rag rug to warm her feet on a cold winter day? Adele's pen flew.

She paused for a moment as a thought crossed her mind. Six months ago, she and her latest beau were in Europe, staying at five-star hotels and dining in fine restaurants. And now she was hoping to find a modest rag rug and eating lentils and rice for dinner.

She laughed out loud at the thought, startling the kittens. At last, she knew which lifestyle she preferred.

Isaiah returned from his first full day of work and realized, with stomach-clenching dread, that his daughter wasn't home.

It wasn't the first time this had happened, unfortunately. But it was certainly the first time it had happened here in their new Montana location. They had barely settled into their rental home. Surely Phoebe couldn't have walked the three miles into Pierce and gotten into trouble so soon?

There was evidence she had taken his advice that morning and done some unpacking and rearranging in their temporary abode. His deceased wife's braided rag rug was unrolled in the center of the living room. Phoebe had set up some of the bookcases, though the boxes with books were still full. She had made a meal for herself, but failed to tidy the kitchen afterward.

They were brand new here in the Montana settlement, and there was nothing around them except farms and fields. With no transportation except her feet, it was a long way to get into town. Instead, Isaiah hoped his daughter would fall in with a crowd of church youngies and make friends.

Biting his lips and uttering a prayer, Isaiah went about making dinner for himself and his daughter. It was risky, he knew, to leave the teen alone all day and expect her not to get restless and bored. He had been too busy today to ask Mabel Yoder if she could find a position for his daughter at the store, but he promised himself he'd do that tomorrow.

It was dusk by the time Phoebe came home. He bit back anger—he knew by now that responding calmly made things better, so he kept his voice neutral. "Did you have a *gut* walk?"

"*Ja*," she replied, and went to the sink to wash her hands before dishing up the stew Isaiah had cobbled together. She sat down at the kitchen table opposite and, from force of long habit, bowed her head for a silent prayer.

Isaiah had started eating earlier, occupying himself with the latest issue of *The Budget*, but he put the newspaper aside. "Where did you go?"

"Just out and about," she replied. Then, to his surprise, she added, "I like the look of this place."

"The settlement, you mean?"

"*Ja.* I didn't meet anyone, but I walked around to get an idea of things. I like the view of the mountains over the tops of the trees. It's very different than Indiana."

"It is," he agreed, resisting the urge to give a fist pump of triumph. Her admission boded well. "Hopefully we'll be able to buy a farm soon and settle into a permanent spot."

Phoebe gave a noncommittal grunt and continued eating the stew. Isaiah scraped his own bowl and went for a second helping. "Have you thought what you want to do? Without a farm of our own, you might be kicking around without any occupation. I thought about asking the Yoders, who own the bakery, if they could find you a position in their store. What do you think about that?"

She shrugged. "Maybe. Or maybe I'll work on some rugs."

Isaiah admired her talent for the craft and did everything in his power to encourage it. She made braided rugs after the style of her deceased mother. "I'm almost a hundred percent certain the Yoders would be happy to sell anything you make in their store. I got a quick tour of everything today, and I don't recall seeing any rugs for sale." He wanted to find her something, anything, as quickly as possible that would keep the rebellious youngie out of trouble. But he also knew he couldn't push too hard or she would push back. "That way you could earn some income," he concluded.

Next Sunday was the first time he and Phoebe would be attending church. He desperately hoped she would meet other youngies in the settlement and not be tempted to seek out *Englischer* friends in town who might tempt her away from her upbringing.

He observed Phoebe covertly over the lit oil lamp, lamenting that his dear wife had passed away when she was so young. He wondered, not for the first time, if he had done her a disservice by not remarrying. It was clear his daughter lacked maternal guidance.

But he simply hadn't found anyone who interested him after his late wife's death. He had no interest in entering into a marriage of convenience simply to provide his daughter with a stepmother.

"Do you want to come to town with me tomorrow?" he

asked her. "That way you can meet the Yoders and talk to them about a position in the store. I doubt you'd want to work in the bakery," he concluded in a tone of humor. "Not with dear ol' *Daed*."

He was rewarded with a brief smile. "You're right," Phoebe replied. "I don't have any interest in working in a bakery. But *ja*, maybe I'll go in with you tomorrow."

It was a big concession on her part, Isaiah knew, but he also knew not to make a big deal out of it or she would dig in her heels and possibly resist.

"It would give you a chance to meet my coworkers," he remarked chattily instead. "A couple of nice women. One works in the community cannery that's in the same room as the bakery, and the other is my assistant baker. She's a strange one, the assistant baker. I can't get two words out of her. It's like she hates my guts, but I have no idea why."

Instinct told him his daughter would be intrigued by a human-interest component such as Adele's odd behavior, and he wasn't wrong.

Phoebe perked up her ears. "How can she hate your guts if she only just met you?"

"*Gut* question. She doesn't have any problem talking with Mabel Yoder or the head canner—her name is Cara—but won't look at me. Am I that scary?" he asked rhetorically, knowing his daughter would tease him about it.

"You can be, *ja*," Phoebe replied with a brief smile. "Any woman in her right mind would run a mile away from you."

It was an old jest based on a happier time when Phoebe was more open to teasing and being teased.

"I'm going to start looking for a farm to buy this week," he told her, changing the subject. "We have enough funds from the sale of our place in Indiana to probably pay cash for a new place. It doesn't have to be big, since we don't need a working farm. Just a few acres, enough to keep chickens and maybe a couple of cows. That's it."

Phoebe shrugged again, her favorite gesture for the last year. Isaiah felt a moment of irritation. While he didn't expect her to stand up and cheer at the news, surely she could muster even the slightest bit of enthusiasm? This would be her new home, after all.

Privately he wondered if he should look at options on the settlement farthest away from town so it was less likely Phoebe would have the opportunity to hang out with *Englischers* that might further influence her away from the church.

Immediately he dismissed the idea. Phoebe's decision to get baptized or not was her choice. He could no more force her to do something she wasn't ready for than he could change his eye color. The thought of losing her to the *Englisch* world, however, was painful.

They both worked to tidy the kitchen, then Phoebe disappeared into her bedroom while Isaiah made some effort to unpack. He heard sounds of industry from behind her closed door and knew she was at least putting the space in order to her satisfaction.

But alone in the main room of the rental house, Isaiah forced himself to confront a painful reality: His daughter was slipping away from him. She was no longer a little girl; she was a young woman, and youngies could often make bad choices. In his mind, refusing to be baptized was one such choice.

How could he convince her to stay? The thought crossed his mind that she needed a woman to guide her. Not a mother—it was too late for that—but perhaps an older woman who might be able to convince his rebellious teen that the *Englisch* world wasn't what it was cracked up to be.

The trouble was, he was so new in the community that he didn't know of any woman who might fit that role, with the possible exception of Mabel Yoder, and he had no idea if the busy store owner might be interested in such a responsibility.

He promised himself to make discrete inquiries at church. Perhaps the bishop might be able to recommend someone.

He was beginning to understand the concerns of the friends and family who had urged him to upgrade his marital status. Apparently they had been able to predict the problems he was now facing.

Momentarily defeated, Isaiah dropped into one of the kitchen chairs and pinched the bridge of his nose. He prayed, "*Gott*, if it is thy will for a woman to help me guide Phoebe, please let me know."

Chapter Three

"Here you go." Mabel handed Adele an envelope.

"*Danke!*" It was all Adele could do to keep from snatching the envelope and ripping it open. Instead, she decorously tucked it in her apron pocket while Mabel distributed similar envelopes to the other workers in the community cannery.

It was early, and she knew by now Mabel preferred to distribute paychecks first thing in the morning. After Mabel returned to the main part of the store, she pulled the envelope out of her pocket, slit it open and withdrew her paycheck.

Receiving payment for labor was still a novelty to her. In her thirty-three years, it was seldom she had money of her own. It was unusual to think she now had to decide what to do with her own money. Living expenses, taxes, charitable donations and home furnishings came to mind. For years, she had never been in need of any physical comfort, but neither had she received a salary for her work. This—this paycheck, this modest piece of paper—was the most honest money she had ever earned, and it still was something she marveled at…

"Are you all right?"

Adele whirled around. Isaiah stood behind her, watching

her with a worried expression. The look on his face—genuine concern—caused her midsection to flip over. Except for her own father, what man had ever looked out for her?

But her sister's warning instantly reasserted itself. She dropped her gaze to the floor and mumbled, "I'm fine, *danke*."

With her head lowered, only his feet were visible in her field of vision, and those feet didn't move for a few moments. "If you're sure..." she heard him say. When she didn't reply, he moved away.

Adele drew a breath of relief. She didn't like her reaction to Isaiah's nearness. If she was perfectly honest with herself, it was the first time in ages she could remember being genuinely attracted to someone, rather than just faking it. It was an odd feeling, and one she wasn't sure she liked... especially as she was on probation.

She pocketed her paycheck and moved to the industrial mixer to begin adding ingredients for the day's first batch of rolls. Isaiah glanced at a chart on the wall, withdrew a notebook from a shelf and shuffled through various plastic-sheathed sheets until he came to the recipe he was looking for.

"Mabel requested some fresh bagels," he remarked. "I'll start the dough, and we can make poppy seed, everything bagels, cheese bagels and plain ones."

"*Ja gut*," she replied. "I'll have these rolls ready by the time the bagels are ready to boil."

She sensed mild surprise from him. She realized it was probably the most he'd heard her speak since his arrival.

"Where do you keep the list of ingredients to order?" he inquired, donning an apron over his dark blue shirt and tying it behind his back.

"Over here." She walked a few steps toward a clipboard

hanging from a nail with a pencil tied to a string dangling next to it. "I write down things I'm short on. Mabel places an order once a month for bulk ingredients."

"Very good." He studied the list for a few moments, then began assembling the ingredients for a large batch of bagels.

For a couple hours, both were busy with their respective tasks. Adele was relieved Isaiah wasn't inclined toward idle chitchat. He simply worked, talking only when necessary to discuss matters of business. She began to relax around him.

Across the half wall of the room, on the side that housed the cannery, Cara and her *Englisch* coworker, Lucy, chatted. Over the last two months, she had pieced together a great deal of information on the two women's lives simply by listening in on their conversations. However she stayed vague about her own past with the other women, merely saying she had been working in the *Englisch* world for the past fifteen years and now was ready to return to her Amish roots. No one outside of the Yoders, the bishop and her sister and brother-in-law knew her true circumstances. She would just as soon keep it that way.

Halfway through the morning, Isaiah suddenly remarked, "By the way, my daughter, Phoebe, will be by around lunchtime. It's my hope that the Yoders will be able to find a position for her in the store."

"I see." Adele kept her eyes on the dough she was kneading. "How old is your daughter?"

"Seventeen."

"That will be nice for her."

"I hope so." At the somewhat strangled note in his voice, she jerked her head up. He had a grim expression on his face, and Adele's impression was his daughter was something of a handful. He met her eyes briefly, and this time it was his turn to turn away.

She felt a surge of empathy run through her. If his daughter was a handful, she could understand. Hadn't she always been a handful to her own father?

She knew Isaiah was widowed and had been for many years. Evidently Phoebe had grown up without a mother's guiding hand. Adele's sympathy increased. She had lost her own mother at five years old and barely remembered her. Would she have turned out differently if her father had remarried and provided a mother figure for his two daughters?

But Adele and her sister had both been raised in the same environment. Yet Olivia had stayed on the straight and narrow path and turned out wonderfully.

While she had fled the Amish as soon as she could and spent fifteen years living a dissident lifestyle, attaching herself first to one wealthy man then another. She had capitalized on her beauty in a way that brought shame to her father, who had been a *gut* man doing his best to raise his daughters on his own. One of the many sins weighing heavily on her soul was that her father had died before seeing his wayward daughter return to the church.

She shook her head to dispel the lingering misery and focused on Isaiah. "What kind of position is your daughter hoping for in the store?" she ventured to ask.

Again, Isaiah seemed surprised that she offered a question. After a moment he replied, "She's a textile artist, you might say. Her specialty is braided rag rugs, but she's interested in all kinds of fiber arts. When she was little, she even bought some raw wool, carded and spun it, and knitted scarves from the yarn, which she sold."

"Wow." Adele was impressed. Her own shocking lack of skills seemed even more apparent. Imagine being shown up by a seventeen-year-old. "The Yoders might be interested.

They sell quilts, but they don't really have any other textiles in the store." *Except my embroidery*, she added silently.

"That's what I'm hoping. Phoebe had—" he paused, and his face reddened "—had some rebellious issues in Indiana. I'm hoping she'll straighten out here in Montana."

So that was it. Adele knew Isaiah had been hired by the Yoders two months ago, but was delayed due to "family issues," according to Mabel. Apparently his daughter was the reason behind the delay.

"If she makes rugs," Adele said, "I might be in the market for one or two. My rental house has very sparse furnishings, and a bare floor will get chilly as winter comes."

"I'll let her know." As he watched her, Adele turned away. She felt like she had already said too much. She heard her sister's voice echoing in her mind: *Keep away from men.*

Shortly after noon, a young woman dressed in typical Amish garb walked into the bakery. Adele saw Isaiah smile.

"Adele, this is my daughter, Phoebe," he said, dusting flour off his hands.

Adele met Phoebe's eyes and felt a shock of recognition. This was the youngie she had seen walking along the road at dusk yesterday evening. But more than that, this was a youngie in trouble. Adele saw, all too clearly, the signs of mulish opposition that had taken root in the girl's expression and demeanor. How well she knew the feeling.

Phoebe was a pretty thing with dark brown hair tucked neatly under her *kapp* and sullen blue eyes. Her eyes widened in first confusion then admiration when she looked at Adele.

Adele suppressed a sigh. Her beauty was always the first thing people noticed. What used to be a blessing now seemed anything but.

"Nice to meet you," she said to the youngie, putting out her hand to shake.

"*Ja, danke*, same here," Phoebe said, returning the gesture. After staring at Adele for a moment, the youngie gave her a genuine smile. It transformed her face from mild sullenness to loveliness. The teenager wasn't as beautiful as Adele knew herself to be, but she definitely had the potential to turn men's heads. Adele found herself worried at the thought.

Isaiah walked Phoebe into the main part of Yoder's Mercantile. The smile his daughter had given to Adele was gone, and the usual sullen expression had returned to her face. His heart sank. Who would hire such a sulky snit?

He found Mabel stocking some shelves. "Mabel, this is my daughter, Phoebe."

The older woman turned, her face wreathed with a smile. "Ach, how nice to meet you!" she exclaimed, shaking Phoebe's hand. It was impossible to resist the woman's warmth and interest, and Isaiah was gratified to see a flicker of a smile cross his daughter's face.

"My hope is you can find a position for Phoebe here in the store," Isaiah clarified.

"Do you have any retail experience, *liebling*?" inquired Mabel.

"*N-nein*," stammered Phoebe.

"Well, we can train you without any problem," assured Mabel. "Though it's helpful to know what kinds of hobbies and skills you have, so we can match you to a corresponding department. What kind of things do you enjoy doing?"

"I make rugs," Phoebe volunteered.

Mabel's eyes widened. "Rugs? What kind?"

"Braided."

"Braided rugs!" Mabel looked genuinely enthusiastic.

"Ach, Phoebe, that's something no one else here in the settlement makes! Do you know what kind of market we would have for something like that?"

"Really?" Isaiah watched dawning pleasure on his daughter's face. "I like working with fabric."

"Do you want to work here in the store or provide us with rugs to sell, or both?" inquired Mabel.

Phoebe shot him a glance, even though Isaiah had stepped aside to let his daughter handle the interaction on her own. "W-work in the store. *And* sell rugs. Both, I guess."

"Hmmm." Mabel tapped her chin. "I have an idea. Isaiah, would you excuse us while I discuss a concept with your daughter?"

Startled, Isaiah had little choice but to say, "*Ja*, sure..."

Mabel seized Phoebe by the elbow and propelled the youngie toward the other side of the store. Isaiah saw the older woman gesture toward a wall. He shrugged and returned to the bakery, wondering what on earth Mabel's "concept" might be.

Inside the bakery, he found Adele vigorously kneading some dough. Her eyes flickered up and met his for a moment before she looked back at her task.

"Mabel said she has a concept she wants to discuss with Phoebe," he told her, simply because he knew she was likely to be curious about what took place in the store.

"What kind of concept?"

"I don't know. Mabel asked to speak to Phoebe alone." He saw the humorous side of it. "I guess she didn't want Daddy tagging along after my nearly grown daughter."

A snort of amusement escaped Adele's lips, but she said nothing as she applied herself to the dough.

He watched her for a moment before going about his own

work. But rather than thinking about what kind of concept Mabel was discussing with Phoebe, he found himself unobtrusively glancing at Adele. He'd never met anyone as shy and skittish as her. And the funny thing was, she was drop-dead beautiful. He would have thought someone with her physical beauty would be oozing with confidence. Instead, he subtly watched the set of her shoulders, the slight hunch as if she were trying to disappear from view. She kept her eyes downcast and her back to him as much as possible.

He also realized he never saw her interacting with Abe Yoder, Mabel's husband, who co-owned the store. He wondered who had hurt her—likely a man. What was her history? Was she widowed? Had she been assaulted?

Yet she *could* open up. He'd heard her chatter with others, notably Mabel, but also with the two women who worked in the community cannery just across the half wall in the same room.

His thoughts were interrupted by Phoebe's return. To his delight, his daughter's eyes were sparkling with excitement. "*Daed*, guess what!"

"What?"

"Mabel said they're interested in having a whole new department open up in the store featuring all the fiber arts from everyone in the church! Not just my rugs, but quilting, knitting, weaving, punch needling, that kind of thing. She said at first it would showcase the things people make in the church, and then later things *Englischer* do, such as embroidering, even lacemaking and tatting. And she wants me to help!"

"Help in what way?"

"She said she would train me in retail work, *ja*, but she's more interested in having me act as a sort of scout to seek out what kinds of textile products church members might be interested in selling at the store."

While Isaiah couldn't help but smile at his daughter's fired-up enthusiasm over the project, privately he wondered at the apparent trust Mabel was placing in the teen. Did the older woman see something he, as her father, could not?

But he would do anything—everything—to support this venture if it kept Phoebe from following the disturbing path she had been treading back in Indiana.

"That's *wunnerschee*!" he said. "And it also means you'll have a built-in market for your rugs."

"*Ja*." The youngie hugged herself with excitement. "Mabel was talking about making a little display area that shows the braiding technique and everything."

"Can they fit all this into the existing store?"

"She mentioned they might be expanding into the space next door, kind of like they expanded to include the bakery and cannery on this side."

"If they keep this up, they're going to own the entire block," he quipped. The Yoders were indeed remarkable business people.

Isaiah knew the couple had started the mercantile in a long-vacant storefront on the town's main street. It was so successful they had purchased the empty building next to it to open the combined cannery and bakery. Now it seemed they might be negotiating to purchase the building on the other side. Currently he knew that building was occupied by an insurance company, but perhaps the back portion of the building was vacant? He didn't know.

"Ready, Phoebe?" Mabel stood in the connecting door to the bakery, smiling at his daughter.

"*Ja* sure." Phoebe practically danced back into the main part of the store and disappeared from sight.

"Whew." He blew out a breath and smiled at Adele, sharing his relief at his daughter's prospects. "Hurricane Mabel has struck again."

Adele laughed out loud at this pronouncement, and Isaiah couldn't help but admire the woman's beauty, for once stripped of her usual skittishness.

"Mabel is a force of nature," Adele agreed. "She seems to be able to grasp the nuance of any situation. I think your daughter is in fine hands."

"I think you're right." He returned to his work, shaping risen dough into loaf pans, pleased that his coworker was actually on speaking terms with him. Wanting to encourage her to continue talking, he realized his daughter might be a good neutral topic. "Phoebe's had her share of teenage rebellion, so anything that can get her redirected away from the *Englisch* crowd she was hanging around with back in Indiana is a benefit."

"She's not baptized then?"

"*Nein*. Not yet. It's my fervent hope she will be soon, though."

"I understand." The shyness was back, and Adele bent over her work.

While the phrase was conventional, Isaiah couldn't help but wonder if Adele did, indeed, understand more than he might be aware. A thought struck him—was Adele herself a baptized member of the church? He didn't know. He knew very little about her, except she was beautiful enough to grace a magazine cover, yet preferred to shrink into herself and avoid eye contact.

Yes, something—or someone—had hurt her.

"And this, as you know, is our latest department," Mabel said, walking into the bakery with Phoebe in tow, clearly giving the youngie a tour of the facility. His daughter gave him a small smile and a brief wave. "Thanks to your *daed* and to Adele, the store now has fresh breads and baked goods to sell, and now we're starting to get some standing orders from restaurants in town. Over there—" Mabel pointed to the connecting facility separated from the bakery by the half wall "—is the community cannery. Cara and Lucy produce canned foods to sell in the store, but the facility is also open to church members who need assistance preserving their harvests too. Ladies, this is Phoebe King, Isaiah's daughter."

After some greetings, Mabel walked back through the connecting door into the main store, still talking to Phoebe, and disappeared from sight. Isaiah watched the empty doorway through which they had left the cannery, and said a silent prayer his daughter might be guided back to the straight and narrow path. Perhaps Mabel was the mentor she needed…

"You're worried about her, aren't you?"

He jerked his head around to see Adele watching him with her remarkable chocolate-brown eyes. It was one of the first times she had initiated conversation with him.

"*Ja*," he admitted. "She's at an age where she's unlikely to listen to anything I say. After all, what can dear ol' *Daed* know about life? I feel like I've been walking a tightrope with her since her *Rumspringa*."

Adele turned to remove some dinner rolls from the rising oven. She began brushing them with melted butter. "She wouldn't be the first youngie who decided to leave the church."

Pain clutched him at the thought. "I know, but that doesn't make it easier. I wish…" He sighed and paused, then blurted, "I've been praying for a mentor of sorts, a woman who can guide her away from her rebellion and channel it into something productive. I don't want to pin my hopes on Mabel, who certainly didn't sign up for that role, yet she seems to be able to pry some things out of my daughter that I can't."

"Mabel is a *gut* woman," agreed Adele, with an enigmatic expression on her face. "And if your daughter is kept busy here in the store or out scouting for talent, she's far less likely to get in trouble." She finished brushing the dinner rolls and slid the tray into an oven for baking.

"That's my hope. I'm also in the market for a farm because farm work would keep her busy as well. And hopefully she'll meet some of the other youngies in the community after church this Sunday."

He knew he was sounding desperate, but he couldn't help himself. Phoebe had been his whole life since his wife passed away. If she chose to leave the church, he would feel like a failure. Worse, he would feel like he'd failed his late wife.

But he clammed up. It wasn't appropriate to discuss detailed personal family matters with a coworker, no matter how beautiful she might be. Besides, it was likely Adele couldn't offer any more insight into his situation with Phoebe than he already knew.

And yet...he sensed a surprising bond of interest between his coworker and his daughter. He wondered why that might be.

Chapter Four

Adele watched Isaiah leave for lunch with Phoebe; he was treating the youngie to a restaurant meal. Adele always brown-bagged her lunch and often ate with her Amish coworker Cara.

"Seems like a nice kid," Cara remarked, biting into a sandwich.

"*Ja*." Adele hesitated a moment. Cara knew something of her background, but not the entire extent of it. "Isaiah mentioned she's not baptized, though. He's worried she may leave the church."

"A single *daed* and a rebellious daughter." Cara sighed. "A tale as old as time."

Adele got the distinct impression Cara was speaking from experience, but it wasn't her business to ask about anything painful from her coworker's past. She hesitated, then dipped a little into her own shadows. "I was like that once," she admitted. "Sullen, rebellious, restless. My *mamm* died when I was five years old, so I don't remember much about her. My *daed* raised my sister and me by himself. He never remarried, though I wonder if he should have." She gave a sigh of her own. "I was always the troublesome one."

Cara made noises of sympathy, but it was clear her thoughts were on the current issue. "Isaiah's going to have his hands full with her, no doubt. I wonder why he never remarried after his wife passed away?"

"I have no idea," replied Adele. "And I wouldn't dream of prying into his private life any more than I would expect him to pry into mine."

"Of course." Cara crunched into an apple. "Seems like a nice guy, though, who's trying his best with his daughter. I hope Phoebe doesn't leave the church, but that's in *Gott*'s hands."

"I wonder if *Gott* could use a little help?" Adele kept her eyes on the food in front of her. "I don't want to interfere, of course, but I wonder if that youngie couldn't use an older friend."

"No doubt she could." Cara's gaze sharpened. "But you'd be walking a fine line. You're practically a stranger to both Isaiah and Phoebe. I don't know how much either of them would welcome outside advice."

"I know, I know." She gave Cara a crooked smile. "It's just so hard seeing someone whose issues I'm all too familiar with."

Lucy, Cara's *Englisch* coworker, joined them at the table with her own lunch, and the subject was changed.

But Adele's thoughts turned inward as she recalled her wayward youth. She recognized the signs of impending trouble with Phoebe and wished there was some way to prevent it.

After lunch, Cara returned to her work, and Adele washed her hands and began making a braided sweetbread that had become a very popular staple in the store. Isaiah hadn't returned from lunch, and her thoughts lingered on the man's daughter.

She knew what—potentially—could lie ahead if the youngie decided to leave the church, and she wished she could warn Phoebe about the dangers of straying from the path—the heartache, the sin-laden lifestyle, the babies being raised by others. Her shoulders slumped at the memory of years of poor decisions. Not for the first time, she wondered if *Gott* could ever forgive her for what she'd done.

She drew in a breath and tried to control her thoughts. It didn't necessarily follow that every young woman who left the church would embark on a life of sin. Most simply adapted to the *Englisch* world without issue. If Phoebe opted not to get baptized, it would be difficult for Isaiah, but not the end of the world. Phoebe was clearly a young woman with skills and talents and enthusiasm. She would do fine.

Then why had she herself gone down such a dark path in her youth?

Almost immediately she knew why. Her beauty had carried her far away from the church, and she had used it as a currency for the finest things life had to offer. But *things* lost their appeal after a while. The exotic destinations, the fine food, the handsome men who came and went…what did she have to show from fifteen years of trading on her beauty?

She looked down at the dough she was working and realized she was far happier here than she had been lounging on a Tahitian beach in a bikini. But working in the bakery and redeeming her life wouldn't bring back her father, who had died without seeing her return to the church…

"What's wrong?"

Startled, she whipped around before she had a chance to control her expression. Isaiah had returned from lunch with his daughter and had walked quietly into the workspace while she had been sunken in misery, recalling the sins of her youth.

Whatever pain was visible on her face caused Isaiah to

suck in his breath. He stared at her for the space of several heartbeats.

Adele felt exposed, unclothed. The look on his face was of intense pity, and pity was the last thing she wanted from her male coworker. Pity implied vulnerability, and she was trying her best to be strong.

She instantly assumed the bland expression she had perfected. "Nothing," she said quietly. She ducked her head and resumed the task of braiding dough. "Where's your daughter? Did she go home?"

From the corner of her eye, she saw him still staring at her. She knew he didn't believe her, but what could he do? After a few moments, he replied, "*Nein*, she's still here. Mabel is showing her some tasks." He turned and moved away to go about his work.

She exhaled a small sigh of relief. It wasn't like she could trauma-dump on Isaiah. He would be horrified by her background anyway, and doubtless regard her with loathing if he knew what she had done.

She instigated no further conversation with Isaiah and instead listened to the chatter between Cara and Lucy, and some of the snippets of conversation drifting through from the store, where customers lingered over products.

She wondered what kind of father Isaiah was to his teenage daughter. Was he autocratic and dictatorial? If so, she could tell him right now that wasn't the right approach to take with a sullen youngie.

But what *was* the right approach? Her own widowed father had tried his best to raise his daughters without the guidance of a mother. He had been anything *but* autocratic and dictatorial. Her sister Olivia had turned out just fine, but she herself had not.

How painful it was when bad choices caught up with

one! Adele ached to prevent a similar situation from happening with Isaiah's daughter, but she had no idea how to go about addressing the potential calamity.

Another factor making her hesitate about getting to know Phoebe was Isaiah. Adele was acutely aware she could only access the daughter by going through the teen's father… and Adele was under strict orders to keep away from men.

But this was different, wasn't it? It wasn't Isaiah she was interested in. It was Phoebe.

Suddenly she had a desire to talk to Olivia. Her sister was three years younger, but miles ahead in hard-headed common sense. Olivia might have some advice on whether or not Adele should get involved with Phoebe's problems.

But she would have to wait until Olivia chose to seek her out. Olivia's husband, Andrew, had expressly forbidden her from ever visiting their farm…with *gut* reason. Several months before, newly arrived in the Montana Amish settlement, Adele had unabashedly thrown herself at Andrew. Adele was so used to men falling at her feet that she was surprised when Andrew didn't fall into that same pattern. It wasn't until later that she learned Andrew had married Olivia in a small wedding ceremony some weeks before. Andrew had been furious at her conduct and banned her from the property.

Another regret she had. Adele blinked back tears of absolute shame at her past behavior. Her sister and her new *hutband* were deeply in love, and Adele was horrified that she'd tried to wedge the couple apart, even inadvertently.

She dashed some moisture from her eyes with the back of her hand and glanced over to see Isaiah watching her with a concerned look on his face. Adele could feel her face redden, and she turned her back on him as she made a show of sliding the trays of braided bread into the warming oven. "I'll get started on the dinner rolls for the restaurant down the street," she said, trying to keep her voice from sounding too choked.

"*Ja gut*" was all he said.

Get a grip, she thought furiously to herself. It was unprofessional to weep at work for something she couldn't change. She didn't want Isaiah to conclude she was too fragile to be an effective partner in the bakery.

This job was her chance to prove her worthiness to rejoin the church. Well, part of her chance. There were many things she needed to do…including stay away from men. And that included Isaiah…even if he was the one standing between her and the youngie she had a desire to help.

Yes, she wanted to talk to Olivia. Her sister might be able to offer not just advice, but some guidelines for navigating around the obstacle.

She didn't know why she had such a strong urge to help Phoebe, beyond a natural desire to spare the youngie some of the heartache she had experienced in the past. But since immersing herself in the Amish settlement so far away from her childhood home, Adele had come to depend on *Gott* a lot more than before. If *Gott* was telling her to befriend Phoebe, Adele wasn't about to ignore the call.

Isaiah shaped some risen dough into loaf pans, preparing them for the second rising. He couldn't stop thinking about the look he'd caught on Adele's face. It was a look of pure pain, of internal agony, before she'd managed to mask it.

He was not an analytical man, but that slipup in her expression haunted him. It was human instinct to recognize and respond to that painful of an emotion. It made him want to offer comfort.

But he couldn't, not without knowing Adele better and

certainly not without knowing the source of the problem. His impression was she had something deeply painful in her past, something from which she had not yet recovered.

But he was new in town and had no close friends he could ask. He also knew Adele was fairly new as well. While she was on friendly terms with her coworkers, he didn't know if she had any close friends of her own in whom she could confide.

He finished shaping the loaves and gave his favorite knife a fast sharpening before slashing the loaf tops, then putting the pans in the warming oven to rise.

Adele, he saw, was busy with the dinner rolls for the restaurant order. She knew what she was doing, and he saw no need to offer help where it wasn't required, so he started a large batch of English muffins.

The bakery was a pleasant place to work, despite Adele's silence. Sunshine poured in through the bank of industrial windows on the south side of the building. He caught subdued chatter on the other side of the room in the cannery. The air smelled rich with baking bread and syrupy fruit smells from the cannery. The bakery workspace was professionally laid out, and Adele shared his obsession with keeping the place scrupulously clean.

In all, he knew he'd landed on his feet in obtaining this position, and he murmured a prayer of thanksgiving for being here, with an added supplication that Phoebe would not stray from the path.

Abe Yoder walked through the connecting door from the main store into the bakery. "*Wie gehts*?" he asked.

Isaiah smiled at his boss. The older man, like his wife, was plump and comfortable looking, with a wispy gray beard and twinkling blue eyes. But his bluff and hearty demeanor hid an extremely sharp mind, Isaiah now knew.

"It's going well," he replied, kneading the dough for the English muffins. "This is such a professional facility, I'm pleased to be working here."

"*Gut, gut*," Abe said. "I wanted to ask you if you'd be interested in attending a house-raising this Saturday? We have a young family that moved in from Wisconsin. They're crammed into another family's barn at the moment, but with winter almost here, that clearly can't last. They have property but no home yet. Will you help?"

"Ach, of course." Isaiah grinned. He loved work parties and knew his carpentry skills would allow him to keep up with the other men. Then he remembered Phoebe. "Will there be something for my daughter to do too?" He wasn't eager to leave her unattended during a long day's work. *To keep her out of trouble* was not stated, but implied.

Abe nodded, and Isaiah saw a gleam of understanding in the man's eyes. "Of course. Mabel specifically asked her if she could attend. If nothing else, it will give her a chance to meet some of the youngies in the settlement, and you a chance to meet some of the men."

Relieved, Isaiah grinned. "When and where?" he asked.

Abe took a notepad and pen from the pocket of his canvas work apron. "Here's a rough sketch of the settlement," he said, drawing swiftly. "Here's the place you and your daughter are renting. If you go down this road—" he sketched "—the property where the house-raising is taking place is here." He marked a large *X*.

"Nine o'clock Saturday morning, and we'll probably meet the following Saturday as well. The family will work on it during the week."

"I'll be there. I'm sure Phoebe and I can come up with a hamper of food as well."

"*Ja gut*, that would be appreciated. The family said they would take care of drinks."

Isaiah always enjoyed the organization and camaraderie that went on at such events. Despite her sulkiness, he hoped Phoebe would find similar enjoyment in the company of some of the settlement's youngies.

An hour later, his daughter walked into the bakery. He was pleased to see the spark of lively interest had returned to her eyes. "I'm heading home," she told him. "Mabel said I could start working full-time tomorrow."

"*Ja gut*," he replied. "Did she tell you about the house-raising on Saturday?"

"*Ja*." Phoebe hesitated. "But I was going to start working on a rug on Saturday. Do I have to go?"

"I think this time, *ja*." He took the risen English muffin dough from the warming oven and began rolling it out. "We're new in town and need to meet more people, so this would be an excellent opportunity. I already promised Abe I'd be there, and he mentioned Mabel asked you as well."

"*Ja*, she did." Phoebe sighed. "Okay, I'll go. But it means I'll have to get started on a new rug tonight. Mabel said she would take all the rugs I can make, both large and small."

To his way of thinking, the more work Phoebe had to occupy her time—and that included attending a house-raising—the better he liked it. There was less of a chance for his daughter to sulk and think about getting in trouble.

"Look at it this way. It will be an opportunity for you to meet some of the women in the church who might be interested in contributing to the fiber arts section of the store Mabel talked about."

He was gratified to see her eyes light up. "You're right! I hadn't thought of that."

"If you make rugs," piped up Adele softly from her work

station a few feet away, "I'd be interested in talking to you about a couple of them."

While she had mentioned the possibility of buying some rugs to him earlier, Isaiah found himself surprised every time his reticent coworker spoke unprompted. He turned and looked at her. But Adele was looking at Phoebe, not him, and he saw an expression of shy interest on her face.

He glanced at Phoebe. His daughter, too, seemed a bit surprised by the offer, but she recovered quickly. "*Ja* sure," she said. "What kind do you need?"

"My rental cabin is quite bare at the moment," said Adele. "Winter is almost here, so I'll definitely need something on the floor for warmth. I'm thinking a larger carpet for the main room, and something smaller in the bedroom. Would…would you like to come over some time to discuss it?"

Isaiah again was surprised by the offer. To have her invite Phoebe over seemed…unusual. But if it meant a chance for his daughter to get some new business, he wasn't about to argue.

"That would be fine," replied Phoebe. She smiled at Adele, one of the few times lately Isaiah had seen his daughter light up—the other time being this morning when Mabel discussed the concept of a fiber-arts department.

At any rate, it seemed it would be up to others to break through Phoebe's shield. Maybe he had been wrong to try to break that ice himself. He sighed silently. Even after seven years of widowhood and raising Phoebe on his own, it seemed he still had much to learn about daughters.

"When would you like to come over, then?" continued Adele.

"I guess I'm attending the house-raising Saturday," replied Phoebe. "So maybe…tonight?"

"*Ja* sure, that would be fine." Adele gave Isaiah a lightning glance and then turned back to Phoebe. "Do you know how to get to my place?"

"*Nein*." Phoebe looked a bit discouraged. "We're still so new here in the settlement, I don't really know where everything is."

"Then let me write it down." Adele gave her hands a hasty wash then seized a pen and paper and proceeded to sketch a rough map. "If you follow the main road into the settlement, you take the third right and go about half a mile. It's a small rental cabin on the left, brown on the outside with a green metal roof and green trim on the windows and doors. It has a small front porch. What I don't know," she concluded, "is how far away it is from your place."

"May I see?" asked Isaiah as discretely as he could. He peered over Phoebe's shoulder at the sketch. "I think not far," he said. He pointed to one of the side roads. "Our rental is here, so it looks like it might be only half a mile or so, easy walking distance." He moved away to give the two women some space, then added to his daughter, "It looks like you won't need to get there in a buggy, which is *gut*, since the buggy is not due to arrive until next week. It's being shipped," he added to Adele, who nodded.

"*Ja gut*," Phoebe replied, picking up the map and slipping it into her pocket. She smiled at Adele. "What time should I be over, then?"

"Maybe six o'clock?"

"Six o'clock. I'm going to go home, then, and start working on a rug." She leaned over and gave Isaiah a kiss on the cheek.

After the youngie left the bakery, Adele resumed her work without saying a word. Taking her cue, Isaiah also worked silently at his task.

Unexpectedly, however, Adele piped up with a comment. "You have a nice daughter," she said, not looking at him.

"I'm glad you think so," he replied.

It occurred to him he didn't mind at all if Phoebe and Adele became friends. He was intrigued by his reticent coworker. If it took Phoebe to break the ice around Adele, then who was he to argue?

Chapter Five

Adele got home from work and gave her rental cabin a brief tidy up. There wasn't much to do except apply a broom to the floor, make sure the kitchen was neat and make her messy bed. She washed the few breakfast dishes and wiped down the counters and kitchen table. The two kittens, delighted to have her home, batted a ball of paper across the floor. She smiled at their antics.

She lit a fire in the woodstove to take the chill off the inside of the cabin, then put a kettle on, hoping Phoebe would feel comfortable enough to stay for tea. She pulled together some tea things, including a fat teapot inside a cozy, and set them on the kitchen table. Then, deciding the room was too bare, she went outside, snatched up a few colorful oak leaves from the tree in the yard and brought them indoors, where she made a centerpiece of them on a tray.

She loved the oak tree, a rarity in a land dominated by conifers. It was a touch of home for her, and now it provided her with some much-needed color in the cabin.

After that, there wasn't much to do until Phoebe came over. Adele went out to sit on the front porch and allowed the kittens to escape into the yard. She took a book and settled onto the porch rocker, watching for the youngie.

At the appointed time, she heard the faint noise of shoes

on gravel and looked up to see Phoebe approaching. She carried a satchel. Adele gave a brief wave.

"*Komm* in, *komm* in," she invited, as Phoebe walked up the porch steps.

"Oh, are those your kittens?" exclaimed the girl as the young felines zoomed up the porch steps as well.

"*Ja*, those are Cocoa and Tidbit." Adele pointed to the different animals. "I adopted them just about the time I started renting this cabin. They're about five months old."

The girl squatted down to pet the animals. "We had cats until we left Indiana," she admitted. "We couldn't take them with us. I miss having animals. *Daed* said I can get a kitten after we find a farm."

"Oh, are you looking to buy a farm?"

"*Daed* is, *ja*." Phoebe stood up but continued watching the playful felines. "Nothing too big, because he's not a full-time farmer. But he wants space to have a couple cows and some chickens and a garden."

"I know there's a place for sale next door," remarked Adele, opening the door of the cabin, "but I don't know anything about it. So...what do you think?" she asked on a slightly sarcastic note as she stepped into the living room.

Phoebe walked indoors and stopped. "You're right, it's bare," she blurted, then clapped a hand over her mouth and looked embarrassed at her candidness.

The room had the living room at one end and the kitchen at the other, with a plain kitchen table and two chairs. There was nothing in the living room except a comfortable rocking chair, an end table and an improvised bookcase made of bricks and boards. The wood cookstove, which provided the only heat to the cabin, partitioned the kitchen and living room areas. The windows had no curtains, nor had

Adele need for them. The small bedroom and bathroom was through a side door.

Adele chuckled. "It has everything I need," she observed, "but it could use a few homey touches. With winter on the way, I think something on the floor would be helpful, *ja*? And it's funny to meet you when I did. I got my last paycheck a couple days ago, and I was thinking it was time to use it to purchase something domestic. Then you showed up, and it seemed an answer to a prayer."

"Well, I brought a notebook to get an idea of what you're looking for." Phoebe hefted her satchel. "I have a tape measure too."

"How did you get started on braided rugs, anyway?" Adele inquired, shooing the playful kittens inside and closing the door behind them.

"In a way, I suppose you could say it was my *mamm*," admitted the girl. "She died when I was ten years old, but she made the rug that's in our living room. I think I focused on the rug so much because *Mamm* made it with her own hands. I m-missed her so much and wanted to do something I knew she would love. I decided to try my hand at one, and rather to my surprise it turned out fairly well. I'll admit I got hooked on making them."

Adele didn't miss the catch in the girl's voice as she mentioned her mother, but she didn't draw attention to the youngie's loss. "What do you use to make them?"

"Wool, mostly. I've tried experimenting with other fabrics—cotton and mixed fibers and nylon blends—and they just don't look or even feel the same. Cotton works fine for lighter-weight rugs that are washable, and people like them for bathrooms and kitchens. I can use strips of cotton sheets for making those. But for a full room, wool works best. Nylon and nylon blends have some stretch to them, and that doesn't translate too well into rugs. I've made a few from canvas and denim that turned out pretty well, but wool is my favorite fabric for rugs, as long as I don't blend it with fabrics of other weights."

Adele was impressed by the girl's knowledge of her craft. "Where do you get it? Wool is pricey stuff."

"Thrift stores, mostly. Back east, I used to scour thrift stores for anything wool—skirts or blankets or shirts or coats or whatever. We moved here with enormous boxes filled with scraps, sorted by color."

"How do you decide color?" Adele gestured toward the rocking chair in the room and pulled over one of the kitchen chairs for herself.

"It's kind of a ratio thing," replied Phoebe, sinking into the rocker. "One color should dominate, whether it's red or green or brown or whatever. About half the fabric used in the rug should be that color. The other half of the fabric should be split between a second color and an accent color. The second color should be about thirty-five percent of the remaining half, and the accent color about fifteen percent. I've learned that's almost the perfect balance. If a rug has only two colors instead of three, then about sixty percent should be the dominant color, and forty percent the second color."

Adele's admiration deepened. For all her youth, Phoebe was clearly an expert. "What would you suggest for this room?" she asked. "I was thinking of a rug in here, and a smaller rug in the bedroom."

Phoebe bent down to extract a tape measure from the satchel on the floor at her feet. "Offhand, I'd say a nine-by-twelve rug in here," she said. "Can you grab the other end of the tape measure?"

Adele obligingly took one end, and Phoebe made rapid

measurements of the size she recommended. "*Ja*, nine by twelve," she confirmed. "This gives you a nice chunk of the floor covered, while still leaving plenty of room along the edges of the room to put furniture and make it easy to clean. Now let's go measure the bedroom."

The tiny bedroom required a much smaller size, about three by five feet, Phoebe determined. She made notations in her notebook.

"What colors do you want?" she asked at last.

"Hmmm." Adele put her hands on her hips and glanced around the small living space. "I like earth tones. Green, brown, red, that kind of thing. Can you work with that?"

"*Ja* sure." Phoebe made additional notes, then gave Adele a big grin. "*Danke!* This will be my first commission in Montana."

Adele grinned back at the youngie. "Glad to help."

A little of the elation left Phoebe's face. "You're so beautiful," she said in a wistful tone. "I wish I could look like you."

Now it was Adele's turn to stop smiling. "*Nein*, you don't," she replied shortly. Then, seeing the stricken look on the girl's face, she sighed and smiled again. "I'm sorry, I didn't mean to snap. I know I'm beautiful, but trust me when I say it's caused far more trouble than it's worth. My sister, Olivia, is as plain as I am pretty, and she is the more down-to-earth person and has the happier life. Would you like some tea?" she added, gesturing toward the silently steaming kettle on the stove.

"*Ja* sure," replied Phoebe. She pulled out a kitchen chair and seated herself while Adele filled the teapot.

"Now." Adele pulled the kitchen chair back toward the table and seated herself opposite. She poured tea into two mugs. "Tell me what's wrong?"

"Wrong?" Phoebe looked startled and a little wary.

"*Ja.* The moment I saw you, I recognized myself at your age. You're restless, aren't you? Restless and impatient to see the world?"

"How did you know?" blurted Phoebe, then made a gesture as if to snatch the words back.

Adele gave a self-deprecating chuckle. "As I said, I was like you when I was a youngie."

Phoebe spooned a bit of sugar into her tea and stirred with what seemed like unnecessary vigor. "I don't want to be baptized," she finally admitted. "But I don't dare tell *Daed.*"

"Why don't you want to be baptized?"

"I want to become an *Englischer.* I want to see more of the world. I want to know what's out there, not stay cooped up with the same people I see day after day."

"Even though you're meeting all new people here?"

"*Ja,* but they're still all in the church." Phoebe looked defiant, and somehow younger and more vulnerable after this admission.

Adele grappled with herself for a few moments, then decided to reveal a little—just a little—of her own experiences.

She sipped her tea. "Let me tell you a story," she began.

Isaiah returned from his first meeting with Samuel Beiler, the settlement's bishop. It was a standard practice, the church leader told him, to get to know all the new members.

Isaiah found he liked the older man. He sensed a strength of character behind the wispy beard and pale blue eyes. And so, almost without meaning to, Isaiah told Bishop Beiler about his concerns for Phoebe's future.

"It's why we moved from Indiana," he concluded. "I was

desperate to get her away from outside influences. But now, I'm not sure I did the right thing. She's been sulky and sullen, though the Yoders—bless them—seem to have taken a shine to her and have given her all kinds of opportunities in the store, from selling her braided rugs to recruiting talent for a new fiber-arts department. But is that enough to keep her in the church?"

"It may not be," admitted Samuel, sipping from a cup of the coffee his wife Lois had offered both men. "But that's the purpose of adult baptism, to confirm a mature commitment to the faith. If Phoebe wants to leave, you can't force her to stay. However, I'll do everything I can to gently guide her."

This was not the advice Isaiah wanted to hear, though he knew it was the bare truth. It was in a somewhat dim frame of mind that he returned home and rattled around the rental house, feeling restless.

He missed Phoebe and had no pressing chores to occupy himself in her absence. It was one of the many reasons he looked forward to getting a farm of his own, so he had some regular responsibilities outside of work.

A farm seemed especially important, since he didn't know how much longer he would be responsible for Phoebe. Despite the opportunities presented to her by the Yoders today, he wasn't sure they would be enough to keep his daughter from being pulled away from the church.

He went about unpacking a few more boxes and making the living space comfortable, but he wasn't planning on unpacking everything. Soon enough, he hoped, he would find a place to buy, and then he could spread things out and personalize the space. Until then, they would live out of boxes for the most part.

But the one thing he had made sure to unpack so it dominated the room was the braided rug his deceased wife had made early in their marriage. Large and oval and glowing in earthy colors, it added instant coziness to the space. Even at nearly twenty years old, the rug showed little sign of wear. The carpet, he knew, was a taste of home for his daughter, a familiar furnishing made before she was born and which she had always loved.

He knew this project had inspired Phoebe's own interest in making rugs, though by now his daughter's skill far exceeded his dead wife's more amateurish work. But it was one of the things that united father and daughter: The original rug would always remain central in the living room. It was a tribute to the woman they had both loved.

Breaking down an empty cardboard box, he paused in the doorway of Phoebe's room and looked at some of the chaos inside. She told him she had plans to start a new project making miniature braided rugs in a variety of colors to showcase her skill and give customers an idea of what the finished project would look like. The idea, he knew, had come from Mabel Yoder, and he silently blessed the older woman for her skill in recognizing the kind of encouragement Phoebe needed.

Encouragement, apparently, he was now too clumsy to provide. After seventeen years of raising his daughter—the last seven years by himself—sometimes it seemed she was a stranger to him.

Phoebe's room was cluttered with some of the tools of her trade: boxes of wool scraps, a treadle sewing machine still packed from the move, spools of stout thread for sewing the rugs into shape. One of the things he hoped to do when he found a farm was to give Phoebe a dedicated room for her craft, including a huge worktable capable of holding a finished carpet so she could sew the shape without constantly crouching on the floor.

It was one of the few things Phoebe had specifically requested, and he saw no reason to deny her the improvement… especially if it successfully kept her attention off the attractions of the *Englisch* world to which she seemed so drawn.

He finished flattening the cardboard box and continued putting the house in order. Invariably his thoughts returned to Adele, his shy coworker, and the haunted expression he'd caught on her face earlier in the day. There was a mystery about her that intrigued him. It wasn't just her beauty that sparked his interest, though any red-blooded male would notice it. But there was something sad about her, and he couldn't fathom what it might be. He didn't get the impression she was mourning the loss of someone so much as regretting something she'd done or still feeling shaken by some sort of trauma. But what could it be?

The fact that she was a woman in her thirties and apparently had never been married was another interesting mystery.

His thoughts were interrupted by the noisy entrance of Phoebe, who came barging in and dropped her satchel on the kitchen table. "I'm home!"

He was pleased to see his daughter's sulkiness had vanished, and she looked bright and excited about something.

"How was your visit?" he asked, moving toward the kitchen, where he was baking an easy casserole for their dinner.

"Great!" Phoebe replied. She washed her hands and began setting the table for the two of them. "We had tea and everything. She's such a nice woman!"

Following the successful afternoon at the Yoder's store in town, Isaiah hadn't seen such enthusiasm in Phoebe for a long time. "What did you talk about?"

"Well, the carpets, of course. She wants two, one large and one smaller. She asked me how I got started making them and had all kinds of questions about fabrics and colors."

Isaiah found himself resisting the urge to press Phoebe for as much information as he could about his coworker. But he kept his tone casual. "What did she decide?"

"Wool, for both. She likes earth tones and wanted something in browns and greens and reds. Brown as a primary color, with dark green and dark red as secondary. And… and she offered me a generous payment on both. I feel kind of funny taking that much money, but she insisted."

"As she should," said Isaiah. "You're making a custom order and should be compensated fairly for your time and effort."

"*Ja*, that's pretty much what she said. She also told me she needed something to give her cabin warmth as we get into winter, and wool carpets would be perfect. I think she's lonely," Phoebe concluded on an awkward note. "She seemed awfully happy to have me visit. I think that's why she had tea things already out when I got there."

"Did she?" Isaiah donned oven mitts, pulled the bubbling casserole out of the oven and set it on a hot pad on the table. "Then I'm sure she wouldn't mind if you visited her again."

"*Ja*, she invited me back. Oh, *Daed,* she has two of the cutest kittens you ever saw. One is silvery gray, the other is orange and white. They're not even half grown, so they spent the whole time batting around balls of paper and playing with strings."

"As soon as we find a farm, I have no problem if you want to get one or two cats," he encouraged.

"If I could find some kittens half as cute as these, I'd love it," Phoebe replied, spooning some casserole onto her plate. She paused for a silent blessing, then poured herself some milk.

As pleased as he was to see his daughter chattering and cheerful, Isaiah wondered how to find out what else she had learned about Adele. So he simply asked, "What else did you two talk about?"

Some of the enthusiasm was wiped from Phoebe's face. "We had a nice chat over tea, but I can't tell you what it was about."

Isaiah's eyebrows shot up into his hairline at this unusual confession. "What, it's a secret?"

"Something like that." Phoebe tossed her head in a gesture of defiance. "She said it was confidential—that means I'm not supposed to tell anyone—and I promised her I wouldn't."

"Well, then by all means don't," he replied. He could hardly be irked at his daughter's promise, though it intrigued him all the more. But he wouldn't pry when the matter was confidential.

However he did wonder in passing if whatever confidential matter had been discussed would be a bad influence on his daughter. As beautiful and intriguing as Adele was, he didn't want to cultivate any influence that might lure Phoebe away from her roots.

"Oh, I almost forgot." Phoebe took a bite and spoke with her mouth full. "There's a farm next door to Adele's rental property that's for sale. I saw the sign on my way home."

"Really?" Isaiah's ears perked up. "I wonder who I might talk to about looking at it. Maybe Abe Yoder, I imagine he would know."

"Maybe."

"Meanwhile, think what kind of food we can bring with us to the house-raising on Saturday."

"Oh, *Daed*…do I have to go?"

"*Ja*, you have to go. Abe said Mabel specifically invited you, remember?"

"*Ja*, she did." Phoebe pouted somewhat.

"Besides, this will be our first chance to meet people from church, including youngies your age. The day after that will be our first church service, and it will make a *gut* impression if you and I are there helping out."

"I suppose."

"I'm sure the Yoders will give me permission to pack up a few items from the bakery," he continued. "I can also make the broccoli salad you like so well. What would you like to bring?"

"I can bring cookies, I suppose," Phoebe said. "And maybe a couple of pies."

"That would be *gut*." Isaiah was sorry to see the sparkle gone from his daughter's eyes. It wasn't that she disliked house-raisings, he knew. Or even that she wasn't interested in bringing food to the event. He suspected a lot of it was the natural shyness that came with being in a new location, away from all her friends she'd known since infancy.

A moment of doubt swept over him. Had it been a mistake, to move to Montana and leave behind so many friends and relatives? Yet he had been desperate to shield Phoebe from the *Englisch* influence that was pulling her away from the church. Would she resent him for that and continue to pull away?

He didn't know. And it worried him.

Somehow, in some way, he had to prevent his only child from slipping away from him. Yet it seemed the harder he tried to keep her safe, the harder she pulled away…and he felt helpless to stop it.

Chapter Six

Maybe it was her imagination, but it seemed to Adele that Isaiah was watching her more closely the next day, now that she had become more acquainted with his daughter. It was a little unnerving. It wasn't that she wasn't used to being stared at by men, but that was during her old life. She was different now. She couldn't—or wouldn't—acknowledge or return the interest. To do so would be dangerous to her future here in the settlement.

What had Phoebe told her father about their discussion over tea the evening before? Was Isaiah's covert observation in response to something his daughter had mentioned? Adele wasn't sure how much she could trust a youngie to keep their conversation confidential.

So Adele spent the morning with her head down, just doing her job. She interacted with Isaiah as little as possible, a challenge considering their proximity.

Yet she wondered about him. Phoebe had mentioned her mother had died when she was ten years old. Isaiah was a good-looking man—why hadn't he remarried? Had he been so fond of his deceased wife as to be inconsolable after her loss? Could it be for the same reason her own father never remarried?

It was with some relief when she saw her sister, Olivia,

enter Yoder's Mercantile with a baby tucked into a sling and a basket over her arm.

Her sister was an expert basketmaker and regularly supplied Yoder's with both baskets to sell as well as to display merchandise. After years of feeling contempt for Olivia's steady and boring lifestyle, Adele had come to admire her sister beyond anyone else.

They couldn't be more different, Adele thought with fondness as she watched Olivia through the connecting door to the store as she spoke with Abe Yoder. It was like she had inherited every possible gene connected to beauty, whereas poor Olivia had grown up plain to the point of… well, plain. But now, married to her *hutband* Andrew, her face reflected pure contentment that brought with it a certain beauty of its own. Adele not only admired her sister, she envied her too.

"*Guten tag*," Olivia greeted, hefting Helen in her arms as she came into the bakery.

Adele dusted off her floury hands and reached for the infant. She never missed a chance to hold the baby. She bounced little Helen in her arms and smiled into the lively little face. The baby examined Adele for a few moments, then broke into a smile, showing two teeth.

"I need to unload some baskets from the buggy," Olivia continued. "Can you hold Helen while I take care of that?"

"*Ja*, of course." Adele was delighted.

"Here, you can use the sling." Holding Helen, Olivia slipped the sling from over her head and offered it to Adele. Her sister had long ago given her instructions on the use of the baby holder, and Adele had become fairly adept, which she demonstrated by slipping her arm through the fabric and then lifting Helen into the holder. She tightened the strap until the baby was snug on her hip.

"*Danke*," said Olivia, chucking the baby gently under her chin. "It will probably take me about fifteen minutes to unload everything and get it registered with the bookkeeper."

"Don't rush," replied Adele with a smile. "You know I'll hold the *boppli* whenever I can."

Bouncing little Helen gently, she slowly paced toward the side of the room where the community cannery was located.

"Ooh, look how much she's grown," said Cara. She wiped her hands on a towel and came over to coo at the infant.

"Oh, is that the baby?" Lucy also abandoned her work and came over to fuss over the infant.

Adele heard a chuckle emerge from Isaiah and glanced over to see him regarding the cluster of women with tolerant amusement.

"How old is she now?" asked Cara.

"She was born May 1," replied Adele, "so that would make her a little over seven months."

"What a beautiful infant," said Lucy, holding out a finger so the baby would grasp it.

Adele shrank inside a little bit at Lucy's innocent compliment. *Beautiful* was such a loaded term in her mind that even applying the word to a baby was worrisome. But Lucy clearly meant nothing by it except gentle praise. In fact, she probably didn't know that Helen was, in fact, Adele's own baby, being raised by her sister.

She closed her eyes for a moment, recalling the stay in the hospital during which Helen was born. The man Adele had been with at the time—the likely father—wasn't there and wasn't interested in a newborn. He had departed a few weeks before, leaving her to bear her child alone. Then she had come home from the hospital to find everything gone...

She had swiftly recovered both her figure and her looks,

which soon enough attracted another man, but Helen was an encumbrance to the only lifestyle Adele knew. So knowing Olivia's steady and dependable personality, she had callously abandoned her own infant on Olivia's doorstep and departed for Europe with her new beau.

So. Many. Sins. Adele whispered a prayer of contrition and opened her eyes to look at her tiny daughter's lovely features.

Cara and Lucy drifted back to their work, but Adele—gently bouncing her daughter in the sling—walked out of the bakery into the main part of the store. The emporium was bustling with townspeople. Some were lingering over pastries and beverages in the coffee shop area. Some were browsing the various goods on display. Some were in line at the cash register, where Mabel Yoder smiled and chatted as she rang up sales.

Olivia entered the store, her arms full of baskets, carrying them in from the buggy parked outside. "Last batch," she called when she saw Adele. "I'll be done soon."

"Take your time," Adele replied, hugging the baby a little closer.

She knew the load of baskets had been whisked into a back room so the store's bookkeeper could inventory and record them. By this afternoon, most would be on display.

The mercantile was a complicated and successful endeavor the Yoders had put together entirely on their own. The town of Pierce had responded by becoming enthusiastic customers and supporters. Abe and Mabel Yoder were generous and big-hearted people, but with a shrewd business sense. Adele was grateful to be part of their entrepreneurship by working in the bakery.

She paced slowly around the store, smiling at the Amish

employees manning the coffee shop, the deli, the pastry area, or restocking shelves.

Now that Olivia was here, Adele decided to see if her sister could find the time to meet and discuss Adele's interest in Phoebe King. Should she try to intervene and persuade the youngie away from her desire to leave the church? Should she stay out of the situation entirely? Adele trusted Olivia's hard-headed common sense.

Finally her sister emerged from the back room, slipping a piece of paper into her apron pocket. She walked over to Adele. "Are your arms tired yet?" she teased.

"*Nein*, this sling is amazing. I see why you like it so much," replied Adele. She dropped a light kiss on the baby's head. "And she seems so happy in it."

"*Ja*, she's a *gut boppli* overall." Olivia's eyes gleamed with amusement. "After my trial by fire," she teased.

Adele knew her sister was alluding to the literal dropping off of Helen on Olivia's doorstep. It was one of the many things for which Adele had begged forgiveness of her sister, who had generously given it—along with a refusal to give up the baby Olivia was now raising as her own.

"I wonder if you have time to come over at some point?" asked Adele. "I have something I'd like to talk over with you."

Olivia's features darkened into wariness. "Trouble?"

"*Nein*, not on my part. Don't worry." Adele smiled, knowing Olivia was conditioned to a lifetime of trouble Adele had stirred up. "Just an issue on which I wouldn't mind some sensible advice."

"Then *ja*, sure. I could probably come over this evening after dinner, as long as you bring home a couple extra blueberry turnovers."

Adele chuckled. She knew by now the store's turnovers

were one of Olivia's weaknesses. "I'll do that as long as you bring Helen." Adele gave her daughter a final squeeze then passed the baby and the sling back to Olivia.

Olivia expertly tucked Helen into the sling. Once the baby was comfortable, she looked at Adele with a more serious expression on her face. "I'll admit, I'm impressed with how you've behaved since coming back to the church," she admitted. "It's not easy for someone to make such a complete and utter turnaround as you've done. I'm proud of you, *meine schweschder*."

Adele felt tears start in her eyes and forced them back. No one had ever been proud of her before. No one. Ever. "*Danke*," she murmured.

Olivia leaned down and kissed Adele on the cheek. "Seven o'clock," she said. "It'll be dark by then, but I'll walk over with a lantern since you're not too far away. I'll expect some tea to go along with those turnovers."

Adele watched her sister and baby walk out of the store. For all the convoluted and complicated history between them, it occurred to Adele that there was no finer person than her sister to teach her to become a proper and respected Amish woman.

She returned to the bakery and resumed her neglected work, keeping her head low and her shoulders hunched as she avoided Isaiah's curious gaze.

Isaiah pulled a tray of rolls from the oven and plopped them onto a cooling rack. He began brushing melted butter over the steaming hot breads. As he did so, he subtly watched Adele as she kneaded a large lump of dough.

He'd been working with the woman for a week now and still couldn't get over how beautiful she was. The rare times he saw her smile—never at him, but occasionally at others in the store—absolutely transformed her into something like a fairy princess from a storybook. To his way of thinking, the demure *kapp* and modest apron and dresses she wore only contributed to her luminous beauty.

He wondered what had transpired between Adele and Phoebe the night before. Whatever they had discussed, he was impressed. Phoebe woke up this morning determined to finish the miniature sample rugs Mabel Yoder had requested, then planned to get right to work making Adele's commission. Anything, but anything, that would encourage Phoebe's creativity while discouraging rebellion was, in his mind, a win.

He watched Adele as a plain woman came into the bakery with a baby in a sling. He soon realized the woman was Adele's sister, and his coworker spent time fussing over her niece and carrying her while the sister brought in an order of baskets. He saw the strong resemblance between Adele and the baby and realized that his shy coworker's genes seemed to be strong in the infant.

He smiled to himself, watching Adele pay attention to the baby. She clearly had a tender side to her.

Late in the afternoon, as he and Adele were cleaning the bakery equipment for the night, Phoebe suddenly showed up. Her cheeks were flushed, and she was smiling.

"I got them done!" she announced in an excited voice.

"Got what done?" he asked, grinning at his happy daughter.

"The rug samples Mabel asked for. I made six in various colors, using a very small braid, so they came out about this size." She measured about eighteen inches with her hands. "Mabel said they were so pretty, I could actually expect orders for just the miniatures, but the samples themselves wouldn't be for sale, since they're just to model what the full-size carpets will look like."

"That's *wunnerschee*," said a voice nearby, and he turned to see Adele speaking to Phoebe, the full power of her smile lighting up her face like wattage. "You're such a talented youngie."

"*Danke*." Compliments were rare among the Amish, and Phoebe suddenly looked shy. She glanced over at him. "Mabel is giving me instructions for my first scouting trip."

"Scouting trip?" asked Isaiah.

"*Ja*. She wants me to talk to some of the women in the settlement about their fiber arts. She gave me a list—" Phoebe fished a piece of paper from her apron pocket "—with the names and addresses of women who make quilts, who spin yarn, who weave and knit and crochet. See? She even sketched a map for me to show where they're located."

"And you're starting this project this afternoon?"

"*Ja*, why not? It's not like I can visit everyone on the list, but I'll start with one. Mabel said my task is to see if they're interested in selling their crafts in the new part of the store once it's open, and maybe even set up a demonstration area."

As before, Isaiah marveled at the trust the Yoders seemed to place in so young a person, but he couldn't deny the enthusiasm Phoebe was expressing. He watched as his daughter disappeared through the door into the main store.

He looked over at Adele. "She's on fire," he observed.

To his surprise, she answered him. "She should be. The youngie is talented. You're a fortunate man, Isaiah. Phoebe is a *wunnerschee* young woman."

"*Danke*." He hesitated. He wanted Adele to continue opening up to him, but some instinct told him not to move too fast. Phoebe seemed like a safe topic. "I'm impressed with how much trust Mabel has in her, to give her this assignment."

Adele removed a mixing bowl from a commercial mixer and plunged it into hot soapy water for scrubbing. "Sometimes it's *gut* to channel energy into passions to avoid trouble."

He was startled, since her words echoed his own thoughts. He suspected Mabel was deliberately steering his daughter into projects to forestall the seeds of rebellion that must have been obvious in Phoebe's demeanor...something he was grateful for.

But it was clear Adele's comment sprang from a more personal source. Had she been in trouble? He didn't know. Daringly, he continued the conversation. "Phoebe said she enjoyed her visit with you yesterday afternoon. She said you had tea." He chuckled. "I think it made her feel very grown up to have tea with an adult."

Adele vigorously scrubbed the bowl then rinsed it and upended it over a drain rack. "I liked having her over. She's welcome anytime. She seemed to like my two kittens."

"*Ja*, she talked a lot about them yesterday evening. I know she wants some pets, and once we have a place of our own, I'm hoping she'll get some cats or even a dog. By the way, she mentioned there's a farm for sale next door to you," he added, returning to cleaning the equipment. "I'm in the market for a farm. Do you know anything about the property?"

"*Nein*. Nothing at all. I've barely explored the settlement, except going to church. Most of my time is spent here at the bakery. I noticed the For Sale sign, but I'm not the kind to trespass, so I haven't seen the place."

"I'll have to ask around at the house-raising then, or at church on Sunday. I have a broccoli salad recipe that's always a hit at such events, although I'll have to go buy broccoli, since we don't have a garden yet. Are you going to Saturday's house-raising?"

"I was invited, *ja*," she answered and gave a wistful smile. "I wouldn't miss it. It's the first house-raising I've been to in a long, long time."

Why? he wanted to ask, but didn't. It occurred to him how little he knew about Adele. Had she left the Amish and was just now returning? Had she moved from back East to escape something painful in her past? He simply didn't know.

But he wanted to. Certainly her overtures of friendship with Phoebe paved the way, but Adele was a woman he wanted to know much better. However, her natural shyness and diffidence were difficult to overcome.

But she would be at the house-raising. So would most everyone else in the settlement. He would lend an ear and pick up as much information as he could about his beautiful coworker.

Impulsively, he decided to tell a small lie. "By the way," he said casually, "did Phoebe mention the dinner invitation?"

"*Nein*." She plunged another mixing bowl into the sink and started scrubbing. "What dinner invitation?"

"She started talking about hosting Thanksgiving dinner. We hosted a couple years ago at our old place, and it was a lot of work but a lot of fun. We don't know many people here, so she specifically mentioned inviting you. She said it's a chance to practice her cooking skills."

"Oh." Adele paused in her task. He was surprised to see genuine conflict on her face—a mixture of interest and dread. "I don't know if I should..."

"Well, Phoebe's cooking isn't *that* bad," he quipped.

She gave him a half smile before focusing her attention

on the sink in front of her. "I'll have to ask my sister," she murmured.

He wasn't sure he heard right. "Your sister?" he echoed. "Was that the lady who was here today with the *boppli*?"

"*Ja*."

"Do you already have arrangements to eat Thanksgiving dinner with them?"

"*Nein*."

"You aren't going to be alone on Thanksgiving, are you?" he asked in some alarm. That would be unthinkable.

"I don't know," she replied with some asperity.

"Why would she care if Phoebe invited you for dinner?"

A stubborn look came over her face. "Never mind. It's none of your business."

She was right, of course, and he knew better than to push.

"Well, *bitte*, think about it," he said with an easy smile. He felt compelled to tell Phoebe he had impulsively pitched the offer in her name but without her knowledge. He needed time to make good the offer. "Phoebe could hardly talk about anything else yesterday evening when she got back. I'm surprised she didn't mention it when she was here this afternoon."

"*Ja*, I'll think about it," agreed Adele.

Isaiah had an inspiration that might tip Adele toward accepting the invitation. "In fact, if your sister and her *hutband* don't have other plans, would they be interested in having Thanksgiving at our home as well? The more the merrier, as the *Englisch* say."

She looked surprised and less wary. "*Danke*, I'll ask them. In fact, my sister is visiting me this evening, so I'll ask if she's interested." She finished rinsing the bowl she was washing, upended it onto the drain rack next to the other bowl and wiped her hands on a towel. "Mabel gave me permission to take home a few of the blueberry turnovers to enjoy with my sister, so I'll bag those up and then call it a day."

"*Ja gut.*" He gave the industrial mixer a final polish. "I'm pretty much done here too. I'll ask Abe Yoder if he wants me to make anything here in the bakery for the house-raising on Saturday. Otherwise I think the only special project we have due tomorrow is dinner rolls for the restaurant in town, and I'm going to start making some Thanksgiving specialties we used to make in my old bakery, including those braided sweet breads in the shape of a turkey I told Mabel about. Also, be prepared for marathon pie making in the next couple of weeks. Mabel suggested a lot of pumpkin pies, but also apple, cherry and even pecan."

"I'm *gut* at making pies, so that's fine." Adele snatched a bakery tissue from a box and opened a glass-fronted case where they stored some of the baked goods that would go on display in the store the next day. She removed four of the blueberry turnovers and tucked them into a white paper bag. Then she turned, briefly met his eyes and muttered, "*Gute nacht.*"

"*Gute nacht,*" he replied. He watched as she walked through the connecting door to the store to fetch the bicycle she stored in the bookkeeper's office during the day. Through the front bakery window, he watched as she wheeled the bike down the store's porch ramp, mounted it and kicked off toward the edge of town on the road to the settlement.

He finished closing down the bakery and shut the connecting door for the night. He was determined to crack open Adele's shell, but it wasn't going to be easy. His daughter seemed to be the best way to go about doing it.

Chapter Seven

At home in her sparse cabin, Adele tidied the kitchen after her frugal evening meal. She made a pot of tea, spread the blueberry turnovers on a plate and put everything on the kitchen table. The two kittens made a cheerful fuss as they batted a wadded-up piece of paper across the room. Adele made sure their litter box was clean. She lit two lanterns and waited for her sister to arrive.

She thought with some envy about Olivia's new home. She had seen it just once, during her shameful attempt to lure Olivia's husband, Andrew, into her orbit a few months ago.

Yet that brief glimpse of her sister's farm had been enchanting. It had seemed like a lovely and peaceful oasis. Adele sighed and glanced around at her bare rental cabin. She was three years older than Olivia, and yet she had none of her sister's mature dignity. Olivia might be plain, but she had so much more than Adele had—including beauty of spirit.

All Adele had was the remnants of a beautiful youth and a desperate desire to change. Oh, and two kittens. She smiled at her pets' antics.

It grew dark, and Adele placed one of the lanterns on the porch to help guide her sister toward the house. Around seven o'clock, she heard the crunch of wheels on gravel and a voice. She peeked out the window. Olivia was pulling a high-sided wagon with one hand and carrying a hurricane lantern in the other. She wore a warm cloak and softly sang as she walked.

"*Welkom,*" Adele said, opening the door. "Is Helen in the wagon?"

"*Ja*, and I think she fell asleep. You want to pick her up?"

"Of course." Adele leaned over the wagon. Sure enough, her daughter was sound asleep, snug inside blankets and lulled by the motion of the wagon over the gravel roads. She gently lifted the baby up and placed her over one shoulder as Olivia picked up the diaper bag from the wagon and swung it over her shoulder. She also picked up the oil lamp from the porch and brought it into the house.

"It's getting chilly," Olivia remarked as she set the lamps on the table and dropped the diaper bag on the floor.

"*Ja*. I'm glad this place came stocked with firewood for the woodstove. Ach, *liebling*, shh, shh..." She crooned as Helen lifted her head and gave a brief wail before subsiding once more into slumber.

"Ah, tea sounds nice," said Olivia with a sigh, spotting the tea things on the table. "It's been busy at the farm. We're buttoning up for the season, so I've been doing a lot of canning in addition to working on my basket orders. We're overflowing with late-season broccoli. Do you want some?"

"*Ja, bitte*, I love broccoli." Half jokingly, she added, "Maybe you should drop some off with Isaiah and Phoebe. I heard him say he was going to make a broccoli salad for the house-raising, but since he didn't have a garden, he would have to buy it."

"Maybe I will," replied Olivia absently. "It's hard to preserve. Do you want us to pick you up Saturday morning for the house-raising?" she added.

"*Ja*, I wouldn't mind it. I plan to bring a fair bit of food, and riding in a buggy would be easier than walking."

"We can swing by around seven in the morning, then."

"I was just sitting here thinking how much I envied you your farm," admitted Adele. She motioned for her sister to pour the tea as she sank onto a kitchen chair with the baby on her shoulder. "Yet I know the differences between our stations in life have everything to do with my bad choices, up to and including abandoning Helen on your doorstep."

"You'll catch up," predicted Olivia, pouring the fragrant tea into mugs. She added a bit of sugar and a dollop of milk, gave the mugs a stir and slid one across the table toward Adele. "And when you think about it, things are improving. Helen is a darling, and I'm pleased to raise her. Andrew and I are very happy. You're redeeming yourself, and who knows what the future may bring? Remember, *Gott* is always *gut*."

"*Ja*, I know that now. I didn't five months ago when I dumped my own baby in your lap. You're doing so much better a job at raising her than I ever could. Oh Olivia, sometimes I get overwhelmed with how much I've sinned." She blinked back easy tears. "It seems hard to believe *Gott* can forgive them."

"But He does. And that's your future. I know the bishop is very impressed with how you've been progressing since you came back to the church."

"Did he say that?" Adele felt her heavy heart lighten. "My hope is to start classes toward baptism by next summer and get baptized next November."

"Ach, *meine schweschder*, it's *gut* to have you back." Olivia's eyes looked suspiciously moist in the lamplight.

"Are you still enjoying the job?" She hefted one of the blueberry turnovers and took a bite.

"*Ja*, actually I am. It's *gut* to work with my hands, and the Yoders are wonderful bosses. I can see holding this job for the long term. I finally feel like I'm *earning* my income, y'know?" She gave a rusty chuckle. "Although I promised a large chunk of my next paycheck to a youngie who is going to make me a couple of wool rugs for the floor."

"A youngie?" Olivia's gaze sharpened.

"*Ja*. You know my coworker Isaiah? He has a seventeen-year-old daughter who makes rugs. She came over yesterday evening, and we discussed a custom order of two braided rag rugs, one for in here—" Adele gestured toward the other side of the cabin "—and a smaller one for the bedroom. With winter coming on, I thought they would be necessary on the floor."

"Strange that a youngie would have that kind of skill," observed Olivia.

"I thought so too, but she caused something of a sensation when Isaiah introduced her to the Yoders. Mabel immediately commissioned her for some rugs and is in discussion with her to help set up a new textiles department in the store."

"Wow." Quiet respect lit up Olivia's face. "She sounds like a *wunderkind*."

"*Ja und nein*," replied Adele. "In fact, Phoebe—that's her name—is something I wanted to talk over with you. She's troubled, Olivia. She told me yesterday she wants to leave the church, and I know it's tearing her father apart. I want to help her."

"Help her?" parroted Olivia. "Help her how?"

"I can see problems on the horizon." Adele fiddled with the handle of her mug. "I can see her making so many of the mistakes I made when I was her age, and all the mistakes that followed. How can I keep her from heading down the same tragic path I did?"

"How does her father feel about this?"

"I'm not entirely sure. I've taken your advice strictly to heart and barely talk to him, except when necessary in the context of work. But it's clear he adores his daughter and is worried about her. And…and I like her. I sometimes think that if I hadn't left the church when I did, I would be raising a daughter of my own. It hurts to think of all the things I missed because of my stupid lifestyle, and I'd give anything to prevent Phoebe from making those same mistakes."

"I doubt she'd sink as deep as you did," said Olivia with brutal candor. "A lot of what you did was because you're so stunningly beautiful. Is Phoebe beautiful?"

"*Nein*, not in the same way. I mean, she's pretty, but not like me."

"Then she's not likely to follow your same path," replied Olivia.

"*Ja*, but I'd hate to see her leave the church at all."

"The problem is, she's not your child," said Olivia sternly. "You've only met her a few times, *ja*? There's only so much you can do to intervene, except to cultivate her friendship. Maybe become a mentor of sorts."

"That's one of the reasons I commissioned a couple of rugs from her," Adele admitted. "I need something for the floor, *ja*, but I like the carpets she makes and I like her. Seemed like a win-win, even if it was a little pricey."

Olivia was silent a moment. "And where does Isaiah fall into all this?" she finally asked with a worried expression. "Could your interest in Phoebe have anything to do with the fact that her father is single?"

Adele blew out a breath. "I've been terrified to even acknowledge him. We barely talk. I feel like I'm walking on eggshells—not because he's said or done anything wrong, but because of my past. And yet…he seems like a *gut* man and a *gut* father. I respect him for that."

"Is that all?"

"Meaning…?"

"Meaning, do you like him?"

"I can hardly help but like him."

"Stop beating around the bush, Adele. You know what I mean."

"*Ja*, I know what you mean." Adele looked at her sister with some annoyance. "And *ja*, I like him. But I'm also aware of what both you and the bishop suggested—that I stay away from men. It's not easy when I work with one. Nor is it easy if I'm trying to help his daughter. He invited me over for Thanksgiving dinner," Adele added on a defensive note. "He also invited you and Andrew, if you have no other plans. I don't know whether or not to accept. I was going to ask your opinion on that."

Olivia shook her head and gave Adele a small smile. "I suppose it's too much to ask you to live alone the rest of your life. Isaiah does seem like a *gut* man. He can't court you until you're baptized anyway, if he's inclined that way, and in the meanwhile it wouldn't hurt to get to know him better…as long as it stays completely platonic."

The old Adele would have taken Isaiah as a challenge. The new Adele was almost shocked at the thought of her association with Isaiah being anything *but* platonic.

She gently patted Helen's back. "The worst mistake of my life was being desperate enough to dump my own baby on your doorstep. I can assure you, *meine schweschder*, that mistake will never happen again. If Isaiah turns out to be the kind of man who might want to court me, at some point he's going to have to know the truth about what I've done. That in itself may be too much for him to take. So *ja*, I give you my word I'll behave as a proper Amish woman around Isaiah. And, with *Gott*'s help, I can help his daughter too."

Olivia's smile broadened. "Personally, I'd love to join Isaiah and his daughter for Thanksgiving dinner. I'll discuss it with Andrew, but since we have no other plans, I think he'll agree."

Adele's heart lightened.

At home on Friday evening, Isaiah followed the usual routine with Phoebe: doing the few chores required in a rental house and making dinner, before a quiet evening of reading by the light of oil lamps while his daughter worked on a rug-braiding project.

While the routine was comfortable for him, he suddenly wondered if it caused a seventeen-year-old girl to chafe. He needed to remember to ask at the house-raising tomorrow if there were youngie sing-alongs or other activities in the settlement.

But he did remember to mention his contrived invitation. "By the way, I told Adele you were interested in having her over for Thanksgiving dinner," he ventured.

He was gratified to see his daughter's face light up. "You did? *Danke!* I'd like to have her over. She's a nice woman."

"I told her you were interested in practicing your cooking skills. I know your roasted chicken is fabulous. Feel up for tackling a turkey?" he teased.

Phoebe actually laughed. Isaiah realized it had been a long time since hearing that precious sound. If Adele was able to bring his daughter out of her doldrums, he would encourage their friendship as much as he could.

"I think you're just biased," Phoebe smiled, "but *ja*, I

think I can make a turkey." She sobered a bit and picked at the food on her plate. "I think Adele is lonely," the girl added. "She's all alone in a cabin that's almost bare, with just the two kittens for company. I—I think neither of us know many people out here yet. Maybe that's why I like her."

Isaiah's conscience stung as her words reinforced his earlier thoughts. "Are *you* lonely, *liebling*? I know it's difficult, settling in a new place so far from home."

"Sometimes, *ja*." Phoebe kept her eyes on her plate. "I didn't realize how hard it would be to move so far away from my friends."

Isaiah refrained from mentioning her friends were what prompted him to make the move in the first place, the *Englisch* friends who were damaging her ties to the church. But to say that out loud would, he knew, rekindle the rebellion. "Well, tomorrow is the house-raising. It's a chance to meet all kinds of new people. Speaking of which, I guess we'd better get started making all the food we'll be bringing tomorrow so we don't run out of time. I have five loaves of French bread the Yoders told me I can bring." He gestured toward a large paper bag on the counter. "And I bought the ingredients I need for the broccoli salad."

"I'll make oatmeal-raisin cookies and a couple pies," Phoebe said. She scooted her chair back and stood up from the kitchen table. "Which means I'd better get busy. We have fruit canned up from last year, so I can make a peach pie and maybe a blueberry pie."

"Both sound *gut*." Isaiah also stood up. "Just think, by this time next year, we might be able to get most of our food from our own farm. I, for one, look forward to getting a couple of milk cows. And if you want kittens of your own, that's fine with me."

"*Ja gut*," said Phoebe, but he sensed a hesitation in his daughter. That baffled him. She'd always said she wanted pets, so where was the enthusiasm now? He pushed aside his deepest fear, which was that Phoebe wouldn't be around long enough to enjoy getting animals.

The unwashed dinner dishes were piled in the sink, and both Phoebe and Isaiah were busy at the kitchen table, chopping vegetables and rolling out pie dough, when there was a sudden knock on the door.

Startled, both Isaiah and his daughter froze. It was nearly dark out, and they certainly weren't expecting anyone. "Who could that be?" he ventured. Dusting off his hands, he picked up an oil lamp and walked to the front door.

An Amish man stood on the porch with a covered basket in one hand. "Are you Isaiah King?" he inquired.

"Ja."

"*Gut'n owed.* My name is Andrew Eicher. My wife, Olivia, is sister to your coworker Adele Bontrager." He held out his hand.

"*Gut'n owed*," replied Isaiah, shaking hands. "Won't you come in?"

"*Bitte*." He stepped over the threshold and hefted his basket. "I heard you needed some broccoli, and we're overflowing with the last of the harvest from the garden."

Isaiah stared, then smiled. "*Ja!* I needed some for a dish I was making for the house-raising. I bought what I needed at the grocery store, but I'd far rather use the home-grown stuff. *Danke!*"

"It's yours, then." Andrew handed over the basket.

Isaiah peeked under the clean towel and saw at least five pounds of the vegetable. "Nothing will go to waste," he assured Andrew. "It's one of my favorite foods."

"That's *gut*, then. *Gut'n owed*," Andrew added politely to

Phoebe, glimpsing the youngie standing at the kitchen table, a rolling pin in hand as she paused in rolling out pie dough.

"I'm sorry. Andrew Eicher, this is my daughter, Phoebe."

"*Gut'n owed*," Phoebe said.

"Would you like a cup of coffee?" asked Isaiah. He instinctively liked Andrew, especially since he was a relation by marriage to the woman who had been consuming his thoughts lately.

"*Ja, danke*." Andrew removed his hat and glanced around the rental cabin. "Nice place," he commented.

"Well, it's temporary. I'm in the market for a farm but haven't had a chance to look around much yet. I got wind of one place and thought I'd ask around at the house-raising tomorrow if anyone can show it to me. Will you be there?"

"Of course, *ja*. *Danke*," he added, as Isaiah poured him a cup of coffee from a carafe. "Keep on working, I don't mind." He gestured toward the kitchen table.

Phoebe stayed silent, shaping the two pies, as Isaiah chopped vegetables and asked Andrew about his own farm, about the upcoming church service and about winters in this part of the world.

"It's a nice place to be," affirmed Andrew. "My wife and I are fairly new here ourselves. I'm from Ohio, and Olivia is from Pennsylvania. Where are you from?"

"Indiana. I'm looking forward to the house-raising tomorrow and church the following day so I can start getting to know people better. But I love my job and feel very blessed to work for the Yoders."

"*Ja*, they're *gut* people. Thanks to their business sense, a lot of us—including my wife—are finding direct or indirect employment through them. And they're well-liked by the *Englischer* in town too."

"So how did you know I needed broccoli?" Isaiah inquired.

"Olivia mentioned it to me. I think Adele mentioned it to her." Andrew sipped his coffee.

"Funny how word gets around, then," Isaiah replied. "I think I just mentioned it in passing while at work. Was that your baby daughter your wife brought into the bakery yesterday? I chuckled because all the women were clustered around her, cooing and fussing."

Andrew paused for an instant, then nodded. "*Ja*. Her name is Helen. She's a *wunnerschee boppli*. Adopted, you know."

"Ah. That's fairly common." Isaiah was a bit startled at this revelation, but didn't think much of it. Babies were adopted all the time. "Regardless, she's beautiful. My late wife and I…well, we thought about adopting too, especially since Phoebe turned out to be our only one, but somehow it never happened. But Phoebe makes up for it by being a *wunnerschee* youngie."

His daughter looked up briefly before returning to her task. She efficiently rolled the pastry onto the rolling pin then unrolled it over the pie pan.

"I understand you make rugs, Phoebe, is that right?" Andrew asked.

"*Ja*," the girl replied. "Adele asked me to make two of them for her for her rental cabin, and the Yoders are going to start carrying them in the store."

"My wife tells me you're very talented. I might be in the market for one of them myself," said Andrew. "No rush, but it would be nice to have a small carpet in our bedroom, especially with winter coming on."

Phoebe nodded. "Suddenly I have a lot of work to do, it seems."

"But that's a *gut* thing, *ja liebling*?" said Isaiah. "It keeps you busy and brings in income." *And keeps you out of trouble*, he added silently.

"The Yoders are *gut* at picking up talent in the settlement. My wife is a basketmaker," remarked Andrew. He gestured toward the basket of broccoli. "That's one of hers there."

"Do you need it back?" Isaiah reached for another head of the vegetable, which he proceeded to chop.

"*Ja*, but there's no rush. Any time will do. We have no shortage of baskets," he chuckled. Then he rose, drained the remainder of the coffee from his mug and placed it in the sink. "And on that note, I'd best be going. I promised to watch the *boppli* while Olivia gets some work done."

"Oh..." Isaiah suddenly remembered his impromptu invitation. "I mentioned to Adele that if you and your wife have no other plans, you're more than welcome to join us for Thanksgiving dinner."

Andrew smiled. "My wife mentioned that, so *danke*. We'd like that. What can we bring?"

"We'll make the turkey, so bring whatever side dishes you're fond of." Isaiah grinned. "Nothing with broccoli, though. It seems we'll have enough."

Andrew chuckled and donned his hat. "Thanksgiving meals should be shared, so I appreciate the invitation."

"*Danke* for stopping in, and for the broccoli," said Isaiah, wiping his hands on a towel and reaching out to shake Andrew's hand. "I can return the basket at the house-raising tomorrow."

"*Ja gut*. See you tomorrow." Andrew disappeared through the front door, and Isaiah watched as the darkness of the evening swallowed him up.

He closed the door. "That was an interesting visit," he

remarked to Phoebe, returning to the kitchen table and picking up his chopping knife. "Visiting a stranger with a basket of broccoli seems like an unusual thing to do. Still, nice man."

He couldn't shake the impression that Andrew had been scoping him out, and then he wondered why he thought that at all.

Chapter Eight

Adele rose well before dawn on Saturday morning to make food for the house-raising party. By this point, she knew how to make biscuits that were so airy and delicious they were in high demand at the Yoders' store. She planned to make six dozen and transport them in an insulated carrier borrowed from the bakery to keep them warm. She also made a potato salad and a green salad.

She was pleased to be able to contribute something to the community event. She rolled and cut the biscuits as the kittens scampered around the room.

A year ago, she had been dining in five-star restaurants with one of her beaus. Which one was it, Richard or Dale? The succession of men was starting to blur. She honestly didn't know which one was Helen's father. "*Gott* forgive me," she whispered, and blinked back tears.

Now here she was, in a sparsely furnished cabin instead of elegant hotels, making a batch of humble biscuits instead of being served lobster bisque and parmesan-glazed chicken with truffles.

She glanced at the small bookcase at the other side of the room. It contained a photo album, remnants of a time when she documented her travels. The volume was a painful mix of joy and sorrow. Joy because it had been amazing to experience some of the wonders of the world, and sorrow because of how she was able to achieve those experiences. She kept wondering if she should just discard the album since she had left that lifestyle behind her, but couldn't quite make herself throw it away.

By the time the sun rose and her sister and brother-in-law drove up in the wagon, the food was packed in a large hamper, the kittens were fed, and she was ready to spend the day helping with the house-raising by providing food and drinks for the hardworking men.

"*Guder mariye*," she greeted her relatives as she lifted the hamper into the back of the wagon.

"*Guder mariye*," they replied in unison, then Andrew added, "Need help?"

"*Nein*. Just give me a moment." She boosted herself into the back of the wagon and settled herself amidst a clutter of tools, a toolbox, a tool belt, a diaper bag and one of Olivia's beautiful baskets also packed with food.

Helen was cradled in Olivia's arms. "I'll hold her," offered Adele.

"*Ja* sure." Olivia transferred the infant into Adele's willing arms, and she settled cross-legged with her back against the diaper bag.

"Ready?" asked Andrew.

"Ready." Making sure the baby was secure, she waited for the slight jolt as her brother-in-law clucked to the horse and started down the road.

Adele covertly studied Andrew, wondering if he was still angry with her after her inappropriate behavior several months ago. She hoped he would relent at some point, for the simple reason it was easier to visit Olivia and her daughter at their home than elsewhere.

But it was her own fault. Ever since, Andrew had behaved politely and never referenced that shameful moment, but it still made Adele's cheeks burn when she thought of it.

Helen was quiet in her arms, and Adele watched the passing scenery as the horse clip-clopped down the gravel road toward their destination. She saw other wagons heading in the same direction, and by the time Andrew turned the horse up a dirt driveway, she was able to see the turnout for the day's event was excellent. It seemed almost everyone was there—the men armed with tool belts and toolboxes, the women carrying hampers of food. Children scampered around, laughing and playing. Women were setting up trestle tables, and men were clustering around a large table where plans were laid. One man seemed to be in charge of the operations.

"That's Adam Chupp," explained Olivia, pointing. "He's the best builder in the settlement and usually takes charge of blueprints and plans."

"Is that an *Englischer* youngie?" Adele asked in surprise, noticing a young man dressed in jeans and a flannel shirt, standing with the group of men and listening intently to Adam's directions.

"*Ja*, his name is Jeremy. He works for Adam." Olivia gave a soft cluck of concern. "His family lives in town, and from what I gather they're not the nicest people. He had a rough childhood. I think Adam saved him from a life of delinquency by offering him a job. He's turned into a *gut* young man, hardworking and dependable. He's well-liked."

Adele forgot about the *Englischer* as she saw Isaiah drive up with Phoebe in a small buggy. He was attired in a dark blue shirt while Phoebe wore a wine-colored dress under her apron. Immediately Adele ducked her head down, looking at Helen's precious face, pretending her heart hadn't started thumping.

Andrew pulled up to the area where wagons and buggies were being unhitched and the horses haltered and put in a fenced pasture for the day. Olivia climbed down from the wagon, slipped her arm through the sling and reached for Helen. "I'll take her," she offered. "Can you handle both hampers of food?"

"I think so, *ja*."

The scene was a familiar one to Adele, though it had been years since she'd been part of the happy industry and orderly chaos that characterized the construction of a building. Hands full, she followed Olivia toward the bevy of women setting out food, supervising children, putting dishes on tables and setting up quilting frames.

She was warmly welcomed by the women, and she was relaxed enough to chatter with them as she helped unpack the hampers. Her heart swelled with gratitude at their acceptance and friendship. It had been a long time since she'd deliberately cultivated friendships with other women, and she was grateful this group didn't hold her past—or what they knew of it—against her.

Within half an hour, the men had their assigned tasks, and the sound of hammering and sawing commenced.

"Can I help?" asked a shy voice at Adele's elbow.

Adele turned and saw Phoebe, looking a bit lost. "Of course, *liebling*!" she exclaimed. "There's plenty to do. I've set myself up to be the dishwasher until lunch time, taking care of all the dirty glasses as they come back. Would you like to help deliver lemonade to the workers?"

"*Ja* sure."

"There are some wagons over there, with beverage coolers of lemonade and plenty of glasses. See that lady there? Her name is Eva Hostetler, and she'll direct you where to go."

Phoebe trotted off to make herself useful, and Adele

smiled at the youngie. She knew the teen must feel awkward being amongst a crowd of strangers, but she knew Eva had a knack for making anyone feel comfortable.

She herself preferred to stay away from the men, instead burying herself at the dishwashing station. This early in the day there wasn't much to do, and she found herself seeking out Isaiah's blue shirt.

She watched covertly as he listened to the instructions from the foreman. Later, he seemed to be assigned to building trusses, and she snatched moments to admire his physique and his skills with a hammer. She kept her glances unobtrusive, since she didn't want to draw any attention to herself.

It felt strange to have her sister's offhand blessing on a possible courtship between her and Isaiah. She knew he was attracted to her, but would he be repulsed once he found out about her past? Could any respectable Amish man overlook the fact that she had lived, essentially, as a "kept woman" for fifteen years?

She watched as Phoebe pulled the wagon with the cooler of lemonade around to the working men, dispensing glasses of lemonade wherever required. The youngie looked fresh and pretty, and she saw a few side glances among the older teen boys working alongside the men.

One teen in particular seemed captivated by Phoebe. Adele saw the *Englischer* Jeremy do a double take when he saw her, and he stared at her for a few moments before returning to his work. Watching him for a few more minutes, she saw he glanced at Phoebe frequently.

Adele frowned. She knew where that kind of interest might lead. Phoebe was too young for marriage, though of course old enough to notice boys. But Jeremy was an *En-*

glischer, and though he seemed to be a couple years older than Phoebe, he was also too young for marriage.

She was skittish about where such interest could lead. She knew that trouble all too well.

It's like I'm her mother, she thought, and tried to relax. As much as she liked Phoebe, she was *not* her mother and had no say in the youngie's activities. That was something for Isaiah to handle.

Phoebe returned to the drink station to fill up on more lemonade. Adele washed glasses and set them to drain and dry. The work party was in full swing. The sun rose in the clear November sky, offering scanty warmth, and the house began to take shape under the men's skillful hands.

Adele glanced over and picked out Isaiah, now helping hoist a truss onto the framed-up walls of the house. At that moment, he glanced over and locked eyes with her. She blushed and turned away.

After working indoors at the bakery all day, Isaiah enjoyed using his muscles in carpentry work. He hadn't met most of the men in the settlement yet, and he enjoyed their camaraderie as they welcomed him during the course of the day's work.

He kept a distant eye on Phoebe and was gratified to see Adele had taken the youngie under her wing. The girl, along with several other young women, was assigned the task of pulling wagons of lemonade around to the working men and providing beverage breaks.

"It's always best to meet new people when you have something concrete to do, *ja liebling*?" he remarked when it was his turn for a glass of lemonade.

"*Ja*," she replied. "I've met a few girls my age too. One invited me over next week."

"Ach, that's *gut*, then." Delighted, he drained his glass and placed it in the basket for that purpose, while his daughter trundled to the next worker.

He noticed Adele didn't mingle with the men. At all. During lunch, when the hungry men sat down for the meal and the women went around filling drinks and resupplying food, she kept to herself, washing dishes.

She didn't seem unhappy—he saw her laughing and chattering with the other women—but she avoided the men. He saw men watching her, though. It could hardly be helped. It wasn't every day that someone as model beautiful as Adele graced a church gathering.

He wondered, not for the first time, what caused her skittishness and shyness. What kind of trauma did she have in her past? He wondered if he would ever find out.

"Ach, this feels *gut*," he remarked to one of his fellow carpenters, a man named Matthew Miller, as they finished a truss and started the process of hoisting it into position. "I'm glad to be here in this new settlement."

"*Ja*, we're *all* fairly new here in Montana," Matthew replied, then grinned. "You're just the newest."

"One of the things I thought I'd do today, and tomorrow after church, is to ask about farms for sale. I got wind of one, but haven't looked at it yet."

"How big a place do you need?" asked Matthew. "Are you farming full time? That would be hard with the bakery job."

"*Nein*, I'm not farming full time. I just want a place big enough for a couple cows and a garden. Maybe ten, twelve acres, something like that. And it's just Phoebe and me, so we don't need a big house."

Matthew rubbed his chin. "I think there's a place on the southern side of the settlement that might work. I know it's for sale, and I know it's not too big, but I don't know anything else about it."

"Who would I talk to, do you know?"

"You might talk with my *daed*, Eli. He's not a realtor, but he tends to keep up with properties available on the settlement with an eye toward matching anything for sale with the needs of new people from back East."

"*Danke*! I'll try to catch up with him today. Which one is your father?"

Matthew straightened up and scanned the work party. "There." He pointed with his hammer. "He's wearing a green shirt and supervising some of the younger boys on basic carpentry skills."

Isaiah made a mental note of Eli's face. "I'll ask him when I have a chance. Ready?" He braced himself along with Matthew and some other men to hoist the truss into place.

At one point, steadying the truss while Matthew drove in screws, he glanced over to the area where Adele was washing dishes. She locked eyes with him for a few heartbeats before he saw her cheeks stain red and she looked away.

The trivial incident impacted him more deeply than it should. It implied she'd been watching him, just as he'd been watching her. Could it be she harbored an interest in him that something prevented her from following up on?

He thought about that cryptic comment she'd made after he issued the dinner invitation: "I'll have to ask my sister." What hold did her sister have on her over something as innocent as a dinner invitation? When questioned, she'd told him it was none of his business.

But he realized his thoughts about Adele were starting to coalesce into something more serious than simple curiosity about a coworker. He was single. She was single. He was lonely. Phoebe hinted that Adele was lonely too. What could be more logical than to think about courting her at some future point and creating a family neither of them had outside of Phoebe?

Matthew finished securing the truss, and he and Isaiah began work on another, but his mind wandered from his work and fastened on Adele. He stole lightning glances at her, but her face remained demurely on her work.

When the group broke for lunch, Matthew said, "Let me introduce you to my father. He might be able to fill you in on properties for sale in the settlement."

"*Ja, danke.*" Isaiah removed his straw hat, wiped his forehead with a handkerchief, then followed Matthew toward the older man in the green shirt.

"*Daed*, this is Isaiah King," Matthew said. "He has some questions about any properties that might be for sale in the settlement."

"Ach, nice to meet you." Eli shook hands. "I'd heard you were working in the bakery, but haven't had a chance to introduce myself yet. How are you liking Montana?"

"Very much, though my daughter and I are just renting a place right now. I'm anxious to find a place to buy, and Matthew here said you might be the best person to talk to."

"*Ja*, probably. *Komm*, let's get some lunch, then sit with me, and I'll tell you what I know."

Fifteen minutes later, Isaiah found himself seated with a group of men, including Eli. After a silent prayer over the food, he reached hungrily for some cold fried chicken. "So tell me what properties are for sale."

"First tell me what price you're looking at, as well as size, location, that kind of thing," Eli replied.

"I don't have a location in mind since I don't know the layout of the settlement very well. I'm looking for something fairly small, probably no larger than fifteen acres, and it could be quite a bit smaller than that. I plan to continue working in the bakery, so all I need is a place with enough space for a couple of cows and a garden." Isaiah mentioned the budget he had in mind.

"Hmm." Eli gulped a glass of cold milk and wiped his mouth with the back of his hand. "There are two full-size farms available, more or less on opposite sides of the settlement, but as they're on the order of sixty acres each, that's too large for you. But there's a twelve-acre farm that might fit your needs. It has a house, but it's fairly run-down, as is the barn. It seems you have the carpentry skills needed to make improvements, though."

"*Ja*, that sounds just like what I'm interested in." Isaiah grinned. "I'm used to making home improvements, so I'm not afraid of a challenge. Is the house habitable?"

"*Ja*, of course. It's just not *pretty*." Eli grinned. "It's an older board-and-batten number, kind of small, but the roof is sound and that's half the battle. It hasn't been lived in for a number of years, certainly since the church bought up this ranch. I gather it used to be a caretaker's or ranch hand's home or something. Do you want to see it?"

"Absolutely." Isaiah hesitated. "Today is too busy, and of course I'm in the bakery during the week. What about tomorrow after church?"

"Technically, looking at a farm is not 'working,'" teased Eli. "I think the Lord will forgive us if we go walk around it on the Sabbath. Shall I pick you up?"

"*Ja, bitte*. I'd like to bring my daughter, Phoebe, too."

"Of course."

Isaiah conversed with the rest of the men over lunch, then resumed working on the house, which was beginning to take shape under the skillful hands of the carpenters.

But his mind was buzzing with the possibility of finding a farm to buy. If this place was as Eli described, it might be just what he was looking for.

He glanced over and spotted Phoebe gathering dishes from the trestle tables after the women and younger children had finished their meal. The women buzzed around, washing dishes, repacking hampers and baskets, and setting up the quilting frames that would occupy many of them during the afternoon.

Adele, he saw, was still washing dishes. It seemed she had hardly moved from her position the whole day. Yet she seemed not to mind, talking animatedly with the other women. He took a moment to appreciate the sheer beauty of her face, especially when it was lit up with a smile.

Then he noticed something. The *Englischer* working alongside the other men, whom he now knew was called Jeremy, kept looked over at Phoebe. His daughter seemed oblivious to the young man's interest.

Isaiah frowned. It wasn't that he had anything against Jeremy, except that the young man was an *Englischer*. Isaiah didn't want his daughter having any more temptations away from the church.

But there was only so much he could do about it. Phoebe must decide her own future. It wasn't like he could lock her up and throw away the key or force her to be baptized, which went against the whole reason for adult baptism in the first place.

But these realizations didn't ease the pain in his heart at the thought of his only child choosing to leave the church. He'd relocated to the opposite side of the country in hopes of preventing that possibility. Now that he was here, he didn't know what else he could do to keep Phoebe from slipping away.

Chapter Nine

Fifteen years earlier, Adele had hated attending church services. Now she loved them. Each service she attended brought her closer and closer to her goal of becoming baptized.

She and Olivia sat side by side, with Adele holding Helen in her lap. People were filing into the barn on the Stoltzfus's property, which often hosted services. Across the space on the men's side, she saw Isaiah sit down on a bench next to Matthew Miller, and ducked her head to avoid his eyes.

"May I sit with you?"

Adele looked up to see Phoebe, appearing shy and lost. "Of course, *liebling*!" she exclaimed, and patted the bench next to her. "Your first service in the new settlement, *ja*?"

"Ja."

"It's a little awkward, not knowing anyone. Believe me, I understand."

"What a pretty baby." Phoebe reached out for little Helen, and the infant wrapped her hand around Phoebe's finger and smiled.

Adele hesitated just a moment. "This is my sister's baby, Helen," she said. "Olivia, this is Phoebe King, the youngie I told you about who's the settlement's new rug-maker."

"Ach, *ja*! Nice to meet you." Olivia smiled broadly and

reached over Adele to shake the girl's hand. "I've heard so much about you, and I understand you're the one to thank for the invitation to Thanksgiving dinner."

"*Ja*, that's right." Phoebe smiled but didn't say anything more. The congregation settled into worship mode as the bishop stood to lead the first hymn.

Adele was conscious of Phoebe beside her. The girl sang lustily, she seemed to listen intently to the sermon, and in all ways she seemed like an active and interested participant in the service.

But Adele knew from personal experience that seething resentment might well be hiding under the girl's demure face. Maybe she was just hyper-focused on the teen, but she remembered resenting the church services when she was the same age. Or was she just projecting her own prior rebellion onto Phoebe?

If only she could communicate to the youngie the dangers that came with jettisoning the way of life in which she'd grown up.

After the service was over, the bishop stood up to welcome the newest members of the community. "Isaiah King comes here all the way from Indiana," he announced. "He's working at the Yoders' new bakery. And Phoebe is his daughter, who's seventeen. Please make them welcome after the service."

Both Isaiah and Phoebe briefly stood up and smiled, then dropped back down in their seats during the introduction. After a few more announcements, the congregation rose to their feet, stretched and started filing out of the barn.

"You're welcome to sit with us during the meal," Adele offered to Phoebe.

She was rewarded by a broad smile. "*Danke*. I'd like that."

Outside, Adele handed Helen back to Olivia and went to help unpack the food from the hamper she'd brought. Phoebe tagged along, seeming a little lost amid so many new faces. Adele noticed Isaiah surrounded by a group of men, including the bishop and her brother-in-law, Andrew. He seemed to be enjoying himself.

Finally, lines formed for the potluck buffet, and she and Olivia filled plates, along with Phoebe. They sat down at a vacant trestle table that had been transported from yesterday's house-raising worksite to today's church service.

To Adele's delight, Phoebe actually waved to another youngie about her own age. "Someone you know?" she inquired.

"*Ja*, I met her yesterday."

It was clear the girl was conflicted. Politeness dictated she eat her meal with Adele and Olivia, but the teen clearly longed to join her new friend.

"Why don't you go sit with her?" Adele suggested.

"*Ja, danke*." Without further ado, Phoebe picked up her plate and went to join her new friend.

Adele chuckled as she watched Olivia strap the baby in a bouncy seat so the infant could be placed in the middle of the table. "I don't know who her new friend is, but I'm glad Phoebe is starting to get to know people."

Olivia smiled. "You're acting like the kid's mother."

Adele gave a start. "I suppose you're right," she admitted. "I feel very protective of her. I don't need to explain all the reasons why..."

"May I join you?"

Adele looked up and saw Isaiah standing nearby, a plate of food and a glass of iced tea in hand.

She hesitated, her natural wariness about being close to men warring with common politeness.

"Of course," said Olivia and smiled.

Adele was relieved to see Andrew right behind him. He naturally sat next to his wife, which meant Adele was next to Isaiah.

After their silent prayers before eating, Isaiah asked, "Where's Phoebe? I thought she was sitting with you."

"She saw a new friend she met yesterday." Adele gestured to where a group of youngies sat together at a table. "I think she's getting to meet some people her age."

"That's *gut*!" Isaiah looked toward his daughter for a few moments, and the expression of pure joy on his face made Adele swallow hard. It was clear he so desperately wanted his child to stay within the church.

"Matthew Miller mentioned you might have a farm you're interested in buying," remarked Andrew, taking a bite of potato salad.

"*Ja*," said Isaiah. "He described it as a twelve-acre place, which is plenty big for me. He says the house is habitable but run-down, as is the barn. A fixer-upper is no trouble though."

"Did he mention where it was located?" inquired Olivia.

"I think he said something about Forest Road," replied Isaiah, biting into a piece of cold fried chicken. "But I don't know where that is."

Adele jumped. Olivia met her eyes across the table and gave her a small nod. The property he referenced was the parcel immediately next door to her rental cabin.

She listened as Isaiah described with enthusiasm to Andrew what he'd heard about the property, and how much he was looking forward to viewing it this afternoon.

She had mixed feelings about this development. If he followed through and bought the farm, he would be both her immediate neighbor as well as her coworker.

While Olivia had given her conditional permission to get to know Isaiah better on a strictly platonic level, she was mindful that men were still off limits as far as her redemption and her journey toward becoming a baptized member of the church went.

Adele's problem was that she *did* find herself attracted to Isaiah…and knew in her heart it was a vastly different tug than any of her previous liaisons. For fifteen years, she had traded her beauty to men who could give her, in return, the illusion of wealth and an affluent lifestyle. Deep down she knew it was just that—an illusion—but she had been so caught up in the glamor of luxury that she never admitted it was both sinful and false.

But Isaiah couldn't offer her anything except the respectable life of an honest man. For the first time in her adult life, Adele found that an extremely attractive prospect.

Isaiah was clearly a *gut* man: hardworking, devout, upright and a loving father to his rebellious teen daughter. In her repentant state, it was a combination that was hard to resist.

And there was Phoebe. She glanced over to where the youngie sat with a group of teens. She found herself obsessed with trying to keep the girl from following the path she, herself, had followed so many years before. How could she convince Phoebe to end her rebellion and stay within the church? How could she convey that Phoebe could save herself years of heartache by following the straight and narrow path?

Perhaps if Isaiah and his daughter moved in next door, the task might be easier.

"That's a development I didn't expect," Olivia said in a low voice after lunch was concluded and she and Adele were repacking hampers. "You might have your boss living next door."

"*Ja*, believe me, it threw me into confusion," confessed Adele. She glanced over to where Isaiah and Andrew were talking. "I see myself staying strictly within the confines of my cabin from here on out."

"Well, I wouldn't go *that* far," quipped Olivia. She adjusted baby Helen in the sling and gave Adele a lopsided smile. "You haven't been throwing yourself at him, so right away I can see things are different with you."

"I'm torn," she admitted. "He's not like any other man I've ever been interested in. I was thinking earlier that everyone in my past had something they could give me, namely the trappings of a lifestyle I thought I wanted. He's just the opposite. But don't worry," she added hastily. "I'm fully aware I'm on probation. I'm committed to returning to the church."

Unexpectedly, Olivia leaned over and kissed Adele on the cheek. "*Gott* has a plan for you," she said. "I trust you to listen to His voice."

Both the gesture and the comment startled her. Was Olivia conferring her sisterly blessing on Adele's interest in Isaiah?

She helped the other women put the yard and the barn to rights in the aftermath of the church service and potluck, thinking about what it might be like to be courted by Isaiah.

But then a chill came over her. While she had an interest in him—and she might have interpreted a returned interest from Isaiah—the fact remained that her nefarious past might be too much for him to accept.

She had better not get any hopes up. She was more sinful than the woman at the well in the famous Bible story. While *Gott* might be able to offer forgiveness, she wasn't sure she could expect the same thing from a man unstained by such a reputation.

* * *

Isaiah was almost quivering with excitement at the prospect of buying his own farm. When Eli Miller picked him and Phoebe up in his buggy an hour or so after the end of the church service and potluck, he said as much to the older man.

Eli chuckled. “Well, don’t get your hopes up too much. As I said, both the house and barn need some work.”

“But the asking price is well within my budget after selling my old place in Indiana,” replied Isaiah. “That means I can dedicate some of the surplus funds into whatever repairs are necessary.”

Eli’s horse proceeded at a sedate pace through parts of the settlement Isaiah hadn’t seen before. He liked the look of the area: scattered farms, crops interspersed with pastures, an abundance of coniferous trees, and high above the trees, the tips of the Bitterroot Mountains just visible to the west.

“It’s ahead, just beyond that cluster of trees,” said Eli, pointing.

“I think this is near where Adele lives,” said Phoebe unexpectedly from the back seat of the buggy.

“It is?” asked Isaiah in surprise.

“*Ja*, you’re right,” Eli replied. “She lives just a bit beyond the acreage for sale, in a rental cabin we own. She’s a *gut* tenant.”

Isaiah wasn’t sure what to think about this information. He seemed destined to be thrown into Adele’s company more and more, while still being unsure how to penetrate the tough shell she had built around herself. But maybe if the farm was suitable, he would have more opportunities to try.

“And here we are,” announced Eli. He guided the horse

left down a driveway crowded with ocean spray and ninebark bushes currently decked out in fading orange and red autumn colors. Then the vegetation opened up, and he saw the house for the first time.

Eli was right; it needed some work, but not as much as he feared. The single-story home had a front porch in need of repair, but with handsome proportions. The windows were all intact and the roof looked solid. An overgrown vine of Virginia creeper, with just a few lingering red leaves, twined around the porch rails and climbed up pillars toward the roof, lending an air of colorful neglect to the house. The lawn was little more than a field of two-foot-high dried grass, punctuated at intervals with mountain ash and honey locust trees.

Visible behind the house was an older wooden barn, as well as some smaller outbuildings in various states of disrepair.

Eli pulled the horse to a stop next to the house and sat in silence for a few moments.

Isaiah studied the structures and the layout, visualizing what it might look like once repaired and maintained, and factoring in how much time and effort such repairs would take.

"Not bad," he finally said, and gave Eli a grin.

The older man chuckled. "Well, *komm* inside and see if you change your mind."

Drifts of leaves cluttered the corners of the porch as Isaiah followed Eli up the steps and Phoebe trailed behind.

The front door was unlocked and led into a large room, chilly and with an air of disuse. The room was clearly a multi-use room, with a stout wood cookstove and the trappings of a kitchen at one end and bare space at the other.

"There are three bedrooms," explained Eli. "Two bathrooms. There's a kind of large room in the far back. I think it used to be a bunkhouse or something."

Isaiah moved around the inside, noting no water stains, which confirmed the roof was sound. The worn wooden floorboards beneath his feet squeaked, but none were rotting. The walls needed painting, the windows needed cleaning and the kitchen needed to be remodeled, but it already had a wood cookstove for warmth—essential for the upcoming winter—and he could visualize his and Phoebe's furniture and possessions spread out.

"Is this the bunkhouse room you mentioned?" he asked as he followed Eli into a bare room about twenty feet square.

"*Ja*. This building was part of the original ranch, and we can only speculate what it was used for, but my guess is it was built for ranch hands and then later converted to a single family residence."

Isaiah didn't say anything, but when he saw Phoebe step into the room and take in its dimensions, he could almost see the wheels churning in her head. This room would be an ideal workspace for making her braided carpets. It was spacious enough for a large worktable at a comfortable height, with enough room left over for boxes of scrap wool and her treadle sewing machine.

"Do you want to see the rest of the property?" Eli asked after a while.

"*Ja* sure. Do you want to *komm*?" he asked Phoebe, "or stay here in the house?"

As he expected, she gestured toward the room. "I'll stay here in the house for a bit longer. I'll catch up with you."

He nodded, pleased by her subdued interest.

He followed Eli and saw the barn, which had some missing wooden boards on the sides and some rotting stalls within, but was otherwise serviceable for the animals he wanted to get—a buggy horse and a couple of milk cows. "It's not in bad shape," he admitted. "It seems structurally sound, just needs a bit of repair here and there."

They wandered toward a cross-fenced pasture adjacent to the barn. "That's the property line over there," Eli said, pointing to a line of conifers that hemmed in the far side of the pasture. "Twelve acres, two acres around the house and barn, about an acre in trees, and the rest in pasture, cross fenced once."

"Never been plowed, though?"

"I doubt it. I think the property was used solely for grazing."

"Fine with me," he remarked. "I don't intend to farm full time anyway."

"The perimeter fencing is likely in poor shape," warned Eli, "so be sure to inspect it before you get livestock."

"Of course. Is that a chicken coop?" He pointed to a spacious lean-to fastened to the barn and surrounded by high fencing.

"*Ja*, I believe so." Eli opened the walk-through gate into the yard, overgrown with tufts of grass.

Isaiah peered inside the dusty building and saw nest boxes and perches. "I like this arrangement," he said. "In warmer weather, the birds have access to the yard. But when there's snow on the ground, they can go into the barn during the day."

"It does seem sensible," agreed the older man. "I think the last thing you'll want to see is the garden, or what's left of it."

The garden space had once been fenced off, but now the high protective wire was tangled and loose. The dozens of raised beds were overgrown with weeds long gone to seed. But again, in his mind's eye, Isaiah was able to repair the fencing, install a drip irrigation system, clean up the beds and plant them with the vegetables he and Phoebe enjoyed. "I like it," he concluded out loud.

Eli chuckled. "Better you than me, young man. I'm at the age where too many repairs are beyond my interest. But if you're serious about buying, I can put you in touch with the actual realtor who can start the ball rolling."

"*Ja*, please do." Isaiah rubbed his chin, spinning in a slow circle to take everything in once more. He gave a decisive nod. "I like it," he repeated. "It's not too big and not too small. It has room for what I want to do, and I have the money in the bank to buy it outright."

He and Eli made their way back into the house, where Isaiah was amused to find Phoebe still in the large empty bunkhouse room. "Dreaming?" he teased.

"Actually, *ja*," she admitted. "If we buy this place, can I use this as a workroom?"

"Absolutely," he replied. "I was thinking the same thing. I can make you a worktable here…" He gestured toward the left two thirds of the room. "And you can put your boxes of fabric scraps here, and there's plenty of room for your sewing machine."

He was rewarded with one of Phoebe's rare full smiles. "*Danke!*" she exclaimed. Then she added, "So *are* you going to buy it?"

"*Ja*, *Gott* willing," he replied. "Eli will put me in touch with the realtor. If all goes well, we might be able to move in within the next few weeks."

"And it would mean having Adele right next door."

"So it would seem." He kept his face and voice neutral, since he didn't want to betray any personal interest in his coworker with Eli present.

The older man drove them back to their rental cabin in

his buggy. "I have to go to town tomorrow," he said, "so I'll drop off the realtor's contact information at the bakery as I go through. Will that work?"

"*Ja gut*, absolutely. *Vielen dank*, Eli, for showing us the property." He shook hands with the man and climbed down from the buggy.

He watched as Eli drove off. Soon, he too would have a place to put his own horse and buggy. Soon, too, he would have a farm where a horse—and a couple of cows and a flock of chickens—could live comfortably.

And if Phoebe's enthusiasm for the large room in the old house was any indication, she was thinking about the future—and the future did not include running around with *Englischer* that might sway her away from the church.

And yes, it would also mean living next door to Adele. And that, he speculated, was one of the most intriguing prospects of all.

Chapter Ten

"I understand we're going to be neighbors," Isaiah commented to Adele midway through work the next day.

Adele froze in the act of kneading some dough. "We are?" she said stupidly, then quickly realized what he meant. "Does this mean you bought the farm next door?"

"*Ja*, I've put in a full-price offer as of this morning. I don't foresee any difficulties in having that offer accepted, since the home has been vacant for some time. Phoebe is pleased," he added. "She's the one who pointed out your rental house is next to the farm."

A smile lit up her face at the thought of having the teen as a neighbor. "That's *gut*," she said. "I like Phoebe."

All the rest of the day, she thought about what it would be like to have Isaiah live next door to her. It shouldn't make a big difference, she knew, since it wasn't as if the farmhouse was even visible from her rental. But somehow it heralded a change in her mind. Isaiah would be near in body as well as thought, and that made her nervous.

Home that evening after work, she played with her two kittens indoors then opened the front door to let them explore the yard a bit. She looked in the direction of the farmhouse, invisible behind trees and bushes. With a toss of her head, she made a decision. She'd never seen the farm.

Here was her opportunity to explore it a bit before Isaiah moved in.

It took just a few minutes to walk to the property, through an avenue of brush and trees until the vegetation cleared and she could see the house, dark and deserted. It sat in a sea of overgrown lawn and was half hidden behind an almost leafless vine of Virginia creeper. Feeling daring, she mounted the steps to the porch and tested the doorknob.

It opened easily. She walked inside and closed the door behind her, glancing around at the shadowy interior.

Despite the air of neglect, it was a large and nicely proportioned room, with a living room at one side and the kitchen at the other. There was no fireplace, but a large wood cookstove separated the two sections of the room.

Accustomed to her own bare quarters, she could easily populate this room in her mind. Phoebe's braided rugs would look beautiful here. There would be plenty of room for comfortable armchairs and rocking chairs, lampstands and even a few bookcases. It would be a cozy place on dark winter evenings.

Emboldened by her daring act of trespassing, Adele walked farther into the house, poking her head into three bedrooms and two bathrooms, all empty. At the far end of the house, in lieu of what would be the logical spot for a back porch, was a large empty room. What could it be for?

She was pondering this small mystery when she froze in fear. Distinctly she heard the authoritative stamp of shoes on the front porch. The front door opened and closed, and footsteps could be heard in the living room.

Frantically she looked around the room, seeking an avenue of escape, but there was none. There was a door leading outside, but it was in the tiny hallway close to one of the bedrooms. In other words, she was caught red-handed.

Feebly she darted to the corner of the room in a pathetic effort to hide.

"Who's there?" called a voice, and she wilted in relief as she recognized Isaiah's voice. The feeling was swiftly followed by embarrassment to be caught here.

"It's me, Adele," she confessed, emerging from the shadows and walking toward the main part of the house.

"What are you doing here?" he asked, looking at her in some amusement.

"I got curious," she admitted. "I've never seen this property and thought I'd explore a bit before you took possession. I know I'm trespassing…"

"*Nein*, you're *welkom* anytime," he clarified. He smiled. "What do you think?"

She hesitated. Somehow, outside of work and without anyone else around, she grew bolder. "I like it. I was standing in the living room and mentally kitting it out with Phoebe's carpets and some nice comfortable furniture. I think it will be a very nice home for you two."

"I think so too." His voice waxed enthusiastic. "It has everything we need, and the property is large enough to accommodate some measure of self-sufficiency while I'm still earning income from the bakery. And I have enough saved from the sale of my farm in Indiana that I can purchase it outright."

"That's *gut*, then." She hesitated then asked, "Why did you move from Indiana, anyway?"

He eyed her in the half gloom of the house. After a moment, he replied, "I moved because I was concerned about Phoebe. She was running with the wrong crowd, and I wanted to remove her from those temptations."

"I see." She didn't dare tell him what Phoebe had told her, namely that the youngie didn't want to be baptized.

"Now it's my turn to ask a personal question," Isaiah countered. "Why are you so skittish around me? Is it something I've done? If so, *bitte* tell me so I can apologize."

She felt heat flare in her cheeks. "*Nein*, it's nothing you did. It's me."

"Who hurt you?"

The quiet question made her eyes sting, and she flinched. How astute of Isaiah to pick up on that.

Into the growing silence, he added, "We work together. We're going to be living next door to each other. My daughter likes you a lot. I'd like to like you too, but I'm aware you don't want anything to do with me, and I'd like to know why. If it's nothing I've done to offend you, then what's the matter?"

"I'm not supposed to talk to men," she blurted, then resisted the urge to clap a hand over her mouth.

He glanced at her sharply. "Not supposed to?" he repeated. "Not *supposed* to? Who told you that?"

"My sister," she muttered. "Reinforced by the bishop. Don't pry, Isaiah. I have my reasons."

He removed his straw hat, ran a hand through his hair in a gesture of frustration and plopped the hat back on. "I feel like I'm at a dead end," he said. "I admire you, Adele. I'd like to get to know you better. Down the road, I might be interested in courting you. But it seems every way I turn, you cut me off."

She stared at him. While deep down she might dream about being courted by a man like Isaiah, she realized she'd never expected such a thing to actually happen in real life.

Yet here was Isaiah, admitting as much. She closed her eyes for a moment. "Don't," she whispered. "It would be a mistake to court me. Don't even think about it."

His eyebrows descended, and he looked upset. "See, that's what I mean. You're cutting me off again."

"I have my reasons."

"And you won't tell me what they are?"

"*Nein*. It's my business, Isaiah. But trust me when I say courting me would be a mistake. Forget about me, I'm not worth it."

The anger almost visibly drained from his expression, and his voice was much gentler. "That's not true. Everyone has worth. Whatever happened to you in the past doesn't mean things can't be better in the future."

"I know that now. But the future is something I have to work toward, slowly. And it doesn't include courtship."

"Ever?"

She bit her lip and recalled Olivia's words. *I suppose it's too much to ask you to live alone the rest of your life*. Her sister even admitted Isaiah was a *gut* man whom it wouldn't hurt to get to know better—platonically, of course.

The trouble was, she didn't know how to be friends with a man. It had been so long since anyone had looked at her with anything except a desire to possess her. Yet that was not what she sensed Isaiah wanted. He seemed to want to actually know her deeper.

"Well," she conceded in response to his one-word question. "*Ever* is a long time. I have to go, Isaiah. I'm sorry I trespassed on your property. It won't happen again."

She slipped past him and escaped out the front door, then power-walked back to her own cabin. Dusk had fallen, and she scooped up the two kittens and brought them indoors.

Woodenly she went about stoking the fire and making a frugal meal for herself, but her mind was buzzing. *Down the road, I might be interested in courting you*, he'd said.

Could she do it? Could she allow herself to be courted?

What kind of a wife would she make? What kind of a step-mother to Phoebe? What kind of a mother to any *kinner Gott* might bless her with?

She didn't know. She had callously abandoned her own baby on her sister's doorstep because motherhood seemed too overwhelming. But her circumstances five months ago had been vastly different than now.

Now she had stability. She had a solid job, she was making friends in the settlement, she had a place to live, she was attending church. She even had two kittens. She looked with affection at the playful animals engaged in batting their favorite ball of paper around the floor.

Up until now she had been satisfied, even eager, to coast along on her way toward being baptized. She hadn't peeked further down the road than that.

Isaiah's declaration of interest rattled her for the simple reason that she hadn't factored in such a possibility. Part of her desperately wanted to respond to his interest, but another part of her was mortally afraid it would jeopardize her path to redemption.

She honestly didn't know what to do.

Isaiah stared at the closed door long after Adele left. What a strange woman. She was an excellent baker with an excellent work ethic, but so shy and skittish that he didn't know how to break through her shell. Such a beautiful woman should be oozing with confidence. He wondered about her revelation that she wasn't "supposed" to talk to men. Men made up half the population, so such a stricture seemed excessive.

She said her sister had imposed that restriction upon her, reinforced by the bishop. Abruptly, despite the lateness of the evening, he decided to pay the bishop a visit. He wanted some answers.

It took half an hour to walk to the bishop's home. As he approached the house, he saw the inside cozy with lamplight. In the deepening dusk, he made out the harvested remnants of a vegetable garden, fenced high against deer, located right off the front yard. Hoping he wouldn't alarm them by knocking on the door after dark, he climbed the porch steps and rapped.

After a few moments, from inside the house, Isaiah heard footsteps approaching the door. The bishop spoke through the heavy wood. "*Wer ist da?* Who is it?"

"It's Isaiah King," he replied.

The door opened to reveal the older man holding an oil lamp. "Isaiah! Is everything okay? Why are you out so late?"

"I apologize for dropping in at this house," he said politely, "but I just had an unusual conversation and would like your perspective on it, if you have time."

The bishop looked surprised, but opened the door wider in welcome. "*Ja* sure, of course. *Komm* in."

Isaiah entered the home to see Lois Beiler, the bishop's wife, sitting in a rocking chair with a knitting project idled in her lap. A handsome calico cat blinked at him from a padded basket on the floor.

"*Gut'n owed*, Isaiah," Lois said. "I hope nothing is wrong."

"Nothing is wrong," he replied. "I suppose I'm just puzzled."

"May I offer you a cup of coffee?"

"Nein, danke."

"Is this a confidential matter?" the bishop inquired. "We can go into my office."

"*Nein*, it's nothing you both can't hear. I'm just hoping for an answer to a question."

"Please, have a seat." The bishop gestured toward a vacant easy chair and placed the oil lamp back on the small end table next to his own seat.

Isaiah sank down in the chair. "As you may or may not know, I'm in the process of purchasing the small farm out on Forest Road. I'm going through the paperwork with the realtor and the title company now. The property has been vacant for some time, so I don't anticipate any problems."

"That's *gut*, then," answered the bishop. "I understand it's not large enough for a farm, but if you're working full time at the bakery, it will suit you very well."

"*Ja*, that's what I thought. It seems ideal for my needs. But as it turns out, the property is immediately next door to my coworker's rental cabin, Adele Bontrager. I went to look at the house about an hour ago and caught her looking around inside the house. She apologized for trespassing and said she was just curious to see things. But then she said something unusual."

The bishop's face took on an expression of wariness. "And what was that?"

Isaiah ran a hand through his hair. "Adele is a beautiful woman, as everyone can tell. Yet she's so shy and skittish, it's hard to get to know her. We work together, but she barely says anything outside of what is absolutely necessary for work-related matters. So in the farmhouse, I point-blank asked her if I had done anything to offend her, so I could apologize. She said no. Instead, she said she's not *supposed* to talk to men. I was thunderstruck, Bishop. She said her sister, backed up by you, gave her that restriction. Why on earth would you give her an instruction like that?"

The church leader crossed his hands across his midsection. "If I may ask, Isaiah, why does her shyness bother you so much?"

Isaiah gathered his thoughts for a moment or two. "A few reasons," he replied. "One, my daughter is very taken with her. Two, despite her reserve, I find her an intriguing woman I'd like to get to know better. Aside from her beauty, she's a kind woman and a hard worker. And three, I've been widowed for quite a few years now. It's natural, when I meet a single woman whom my daughter seems to like, to think ahead toward courtship. But I can't make any headway with her, and I want to know why."

"Understand I can't betray any confidences," Samuel warned.

That statement in itself told Isaiah something. Clearly Adele had done something that put her under the church leader's direct consideration. "I understand," he said. "But why isn't she supposed to talk to men? There are a lot of us around, after all," he quipped.

"I need to warn you, Isaiah, that she's not baptized."

"She's not?" Isaiah's jaw dropped. That possibility had never occurred to him.

"*Nein.* She's returning to the Amish after many years away in the *Englisch* world and is anxious to join the church. She has a journey ahead of her toward baptism, and it may be a difficult journey. For that reason, you're going to have to take it slow with her."

Isaiah's mind was buzzing. Unbaptized? Many years away? What happened in those years that had caused her to be so skittish? And why the stricture against associating with men?

"Was she ever married?" he asked after a while. "I overheard her say at one point that she's thirty-three years old.

It seems unusual for an Amish woman not to be married or have children by that age."

"To answer that would betray the confidence I'm bound to keep," the bishop answered inflexibly.

Isaiah fell silent again, wondering. During her time in the *Englisch* world, had she been married? Divorced? Widowed? Had she been beaten or abused by someone in her past? He didn't know, and clearly the church leader wasn't about to tell him. "Then what am I supposed to do?" he murmured more to himself than anything else.

"Isaiah." Lois Beiler rested her hands on her knitting yarn. "Adele is a lovely woman, and I don't mean just her face. But she has some pain she's overcoming. Even if you were interested in courting her, you couldn't marry until after she's baptized anyway, and that's at least a year away, if not more."

"What I don't understand," Isaiah replied with a trace of impatience, "is why all the secrecy? There isn't one of us who hasn't overcome something painful in our past. What makes her different?"

In the brief silence that followed, he saw a lightning quick glance exchanged between the bishop and his wife, and he clearly read a solidarity of silence in their look.

"That's something Adele herself must tell," the bishop finally said. "It's not my place to say, or even your place to ask. If you're truly interested in courting her at some point, you'll have to be patient. But Isaiah, I will say this: Adele has more to her than it appears. You may not want to court her when you learn everything about her. She has *gut* reason to be shy and reserved. I ask you to look beyond her beautiful face to the true woman beneath before you decide you want to court her."

"But how can I look at the true woman beneath if she

barely speaks to me?" He wasn't sure if it was pain or anger that made his voice sound rough.

"Patience, patience," the bishop repeated. "That's all I can say."

But Isaiah wasn't feeling patient. On the contrary, he felt this visit had been a waste of time, though he could hardly say as much to the respectable couple before him. "I understand," he said instead. "And I'll try to be patient. But I can't imagine anything Adele could have done that would prevent me from wanting to court her at some point."

"I'm glad to hear it," Samuel Beiler replied with a smile. "And I pray it's the truth. Adele deserves some happiness, and I'm glad she's returning to the church."

There wasn't much point in lingering. Isaiah rose, apologized once again for the late intrusion, thanked the bishop and his wife for their time and took his leave.

As he walked home in the near darkness, he reviewed the unusual conversation. Despite his frustration at not having his curiosity satisfied, he did pick up a few intriguing hints about Adele.

It seemed she was far more complex than he'd realized. He was correct in guessing that she had been badly hurt in the past, presumably while out in the *Englisch* world. Now he found that whatever mysterious past she had, the bishop seemed to think it was serious enough to deter him from courting her. He honestly could not fathom what Adele could have done, or why he himself was supposed to be repulsed by it.

Well, he had to be patient. He had no choice. But if he was interested in getting to know Adele better, and had any hope of breaking through her shell, he could think of no finer way than to encourage the budding friendship between her and his daughter.

A couple of braided rag rugs, he realized, might have far greater significance than just an exchange of money for a product.

It wasn't until he was nearly home that a sudden thought struck him: Had Adele commissioned two rugs from his daughter because she needed two rugs? Or was she, too, indirectly indicating an interest in him?

It was a vain and arrogant thought, but one he clung to in tenuous hope.

Chapter Eleven

"And my bedroom faces south!" enthused Phoebe. "And there's a big tree right outside, so I'll have shade in the summer."

Adele smiled as the youngie chattered about their new home while she brushed melted butter on some hot rolls fresh from the oven in the bakery. She knew Isaiah and his daughter had moved into the farmhouse over the previous weekend. Phoebe had been busy working on the fiber-arts project the Yoders had commissioned, as well as helping move herself and her father into their new home, and—as she never hesitated to inform Adele—making good progress on the two carpets she had ordered.

"There's this big room in the back of the house that *Daed* gave me for my rug-making studio," continued Phoebe. "He even slapped together a worktable so I don't have to kneel on the floor to sew the braids together. You can see how the progress is being made on your orders when you come over for Thanksgiving dinner tomorrow."

"I know my sister and brother-in-law are grateful for the invitation. Speaking of which, what should I bring?"

"We're making the turkey, gravy and mashed potatoes," said Phoebe. "What kind of side dishes do you like?"

"I have a wild-rice stuffing I'm fond of," Adele replied.

"I haven't made it in years, but it's easy. I could bring that and maybe a salad and some shortbread for dessert. Will that work?"

"*Ja*, and then whatever your sister brings too. We should have a full table."

"What time should we be there?"

"I don't know." Phoebe looked at her father. "*Daed*, what time should we make dinner?"

"Four o'clock?" suggested Isaiah. "It's later than normal, but we're a small group, and it should give everyone a chance to finish their barn chores for the evening."

"*Ja gut.*" Adele's conscience smote her just a bit. She knew the presence of Olivia and Andrew meant—technically—she wasn't fraternizing with a man, but there was no question she had a personal interest in spending the holiday with Isaiah and his daughter. But, she justified to herself, it was just another effort to keep Phoebe focused on activities that might prevent her from going down the wrong road.

Phoebe left the bakery to do some work for the Yoders. But Isaiah filled up the ensuing silence with a stream of light comments, describing the process of moving and settling in. He had seemed unusually chatty over the last couple of weeks, since that awkward evening he caught her trespassing in the farmhouse, and she wondered why.

But she had learned a great deal about him during that time. She learned how he started baking, she learned about his community back in Indiana, she learned his concerns for Phoebe's future. He even mentioned in passing the circumstances behind his wife's tragic passing—being hit by a car while walking on the side of the road.

Adele didn't ask him to reveal these things, but he effortlessly told them to her. He didn't seem to expect any responses, but she listened and learned much about him.

And she wondered…were his largely one-sided conversations deliberate? Was he trying to tell her about himself without the pressure of courting?

His chatter confirmed her impression of him. Isaiah was a good and upstanding man, plagued by the usual concerns of fatherhood, but without many regrets in his life, despite the tragedy of losing his wife so early. How different he was from her!

Thanksgiving morning dawned clear and frosty. Adele started a fire in the woodstove to warm the room, grateful for the heat and shelter of the little rental cabin. She made a batch of shortbread, then chopped onions and carrots to sauté in butter for the wild-rice stuffing. While the dish simmered, she made a hearty Caesar salad.

The dishes didn't take long to complete, and the day stretched in front of her, empty until four o'clock. Adele took the opportunity to do some embroidery, focusing on a fanciful piece of bright autumn leaves punctuated by black crows. She knew Mabel Yoder would be able to sell the piece when it was finished. Being able to sell her embroidery had two benefits: It brought a bit of extra income, and it gave her something to do during her solitary evenings at home, alone except for the kittens that now snoozed in a patch of sunlight.

In the late afternoon, she smoothed and tidied her hair, then re-pinned her *kapp.* For the first time in a long time, she looked at herself in a mirror. Yes, she was still beautiful. Why had *Gott* seen fit to grace her with such beauty? Surely it wasn't to behave as she had done for the past fifteen years. She turned away from the glass and packed the cookies in one of Olivia's stout baskets lined with a clean dishcloth.

She donned a warm wool cloak against the chill of the autumn air. As she walked to the farm next door, she thought of how terribly she had misused her gift of beauty. An upstanding woman graced with looks such as hers would do everything in her power to use that gift for good. But she had treated the gift terribly. "Forgive me, *Gott*," she whispered, not for the first time.

She approached the farmhouse, now warm with lamplight as dusk approached. Isaiah had scythed down the weeds in the front yard into something approximating a lawn, and she saw the overgrown Virginia creeper vine had also been trimmed into something more manageable. The swept porch now had two rocking chairs on it, silently inviting conversation.

Olivia and Andrew had not yet arrived. For a moment, Adele hesitated. Should she wait for them?

After a moment's pause, she climbed the porch steps and knocked. Some hasty footsteps within, and the door was whisked open by Phoebe. "*Welkom!*"

"*Danke.*" She stepped inside and let out an involuntary "Ooohh…"

The home was completely transformed. A thick, braided rag rug dominated the living room, and the space had easy chairs, end tables—one of which sported an oil lamp—and two stuffed bookcases. The kitchen was stocked and redolent with the scent of roasting turkey, with the plain wooden table set neatly with plates and cutlery with a lamp glowing in the middle.

"This certainly looks nicer than the last time I was here," she quipped, removing her cloak and hanging it on a hook near the front door. "You must have been working very hard to get everything in place in this short a time."

"Well, we had incentive," said Isaiah with a twinkle in his eye, walking into the room. Her heartbeat quickened at his presence. "This is the first celebration in our new home."

She sniffed the air again. "The turkey smells *wunner-schee*."

"I hope it all turns out," said Phoebe shyly. "It's the first time I made a turkey all by myself."

"I brought some shortbread for dessert." Adele handed over the basket. "And a salad and a wild rice stuffing I'm especially fond of."

"Before we eat, would you like to see my workroom?" the girl asked eagerly.

"*Ja* sure, I'd love to."

Adele followed the youngie's excited figure to the back of the house into the large, odd room Adele had been trapped in while trespassing before.

This room was also transformed. In the dusky light from the windows, Adele saw a huge waist-high table in the center of the room, covered with an unfinished rug. One wall had a treadle sewing machine, and huge cardboard boxes lined the remainder of the wall.

"See? *Daed* made me this table so I could work on the rugs more comfortably. This is yours," said Phoebe.

Adele approached the half-finished project. She stroked it and felt the heavy weight of the wool fabric. The braids were uniform, and Phoebe was in the process of sewing the braids into the classic oval shape of the finished carpet. To Adele's untutored eyes, the project looked beautiful.

"It's incredible," she said. She leaned down to peer more closely at the handiwork. One end of a braid was unfinished, clamped to a piece of wood screwed to the table top. A thin metal tool with a heavy black thread was alongside. "Show me how you do this."

"Like this." Phoebe fingered the pieces of unbraided

wool. "As I braid, I fold the strips of fabric into something like a tube. When I'm making a curve, I depart from the left-right sequence of braiding and fold right-over-center, then right-over-center, then left-over-center." She demonstrated. "I continue that pattern depending on how tight I want to make the curve. I use this—" she held up the metal tool "—to sew—or lace—the rug as I go. It's called a braid-kin lacer, sometimes called a lacing needle." She pushed the tool through the strips of wool and drew the braids together tightly. "I use unwaxed linen thread."

"Wow," breathed Adele. She was deeply impressed with the youngie's skills and knowledge. "This is incredible. Is that your supply of wool?" She pointed to the series of boxes against the wall.

"*Ja.*" Phoebe walked toward the row of boxes. "See? They're roughly sorted by color. Most of the colors are darker earth tones, including patterns such as herringbone or plaid, but I have a few bright colors such as red or turquoise or bright green, in case I want something to pop with color. I haven't really found any wool that I can't use in *something.*"

"This is the ultimate in recycling," noted Adele, scanning the huge collection of scraps.

"*Ja.* I'll have to put the word out here in Pierce that I'm in the market for discarded wool garments. Maybe the Yoders will let me post a sign in the store or something."

"Phoebe, this is an incredible skill you have," praised Adele. "I'm almost twice your age and could never do anything even remotely this skilled."

The youngie looked pleased. "I have to credit my *mamm,*" she said. "That's her carpet out in the living room. After she died, I started learning how to make these as—as a sort of tribute to her." The girl's eyes got very bright with unshed tears.

Adele reached out and patted her shoulder. "Your *mamm* would be very proud of you," she said quietly. "You've done wonders."

"*Danke.*" Phoebe gave a discrete sniff. "Well, I'd better check the turkey." She moved back toward the main part of the house. "Oh, this is my bedroom." She detoured into a small room kitted out with a single bed, a dresser, hooks on the wall, the inevitable braided rag rug on the floor and a rocking chair.

"Lovely." And to Adele, it was. It was nothing like the lavishly furnished bedrooms she had stayed in during her years of being nothing but arm candy for rich men. There was no artwork on the walls, no knickknacks or tchotchkes cluttering the dresser top, no music posters or magazines or other indications of adolescence. To Adele, accustomed to so many years of luxurious furnishings, she thought the simple bedroom decor was beautiful.

A commotion at the front door brought Phoebe back into the hallway. "Your sister and brother-in-law are here," she said.

Adele felt some relief. She wouldn't be alone with Isaiah and Phoebe. Especially Isaiah.

"Phoebe made almost everything herself," said Isaiah with pride, after greeting the Eichers and inviting them to divest their outerwear. Andrew carried a basket of goodies while Olivia had the baby tucked in a sling and covered with a blanket. "She specifically said she wanted to rise to the challenge."

"*Gut* for you, child," said Olivia with a smile. "We brought many side dishes, so we'll have a full table. Glory be to *Gott.*"

The next few minutes were busy as Olivia and Adele unpacked their hampers and Isaiah placed the dishes on the table. Phoebe pulled the golden-brown turkey from the oven and mashed the potatoes. Isaiah asked Olivia to put the baby's bouncy seat on the table so the infant could be part of the celebration.

When the table was ready, Isaiah invited his guests to seat themselves, and all bowed their heads for a lengthy and silent prayer. Then he stood and began carving the turkey.

"I'm so glad you could *komm*," he said to Olivia and Andrew, and included Adele in the remark, as he plated the sliced meat. "Thanksgiving is much more fun with guests."

"It's our first Thanksgiving here in Montana," said Andrew. "We were feeling a bit sorry for ourselves, not having anyone to eat with, so your invitation is much appreciated."

"Try the biscuits," Isaiah added. "My wife used to make biscuits that were absolutely wonderful. Phoebe's are actually better."

"*Daed*." He saw his daughter's cheeks stain red as she cut her turkey.

Silence fell across the table for a few moments as everyone concentrated on the food. For Isaiah, having Adele and her relatives join him and Phoebe for a meal hearkened back to the happier times when his wife was alive. It was like having a family again, and it renewed his interest in courting Adele, although the bishop had advised him to "take it slow."

Reluctant to pass up the heaven-sent opportunity to get to know Adele better, he directed a comment to her: "I understand you're returning to the church after many years away."

"*Ja*." Adele eyed him warily, her dark eyes looking black in the lamplight. She flashed a lightning glance at her sister.

He ignored her cautious expression and plunged on. "So what did you do out in the *Englisch* world?"

"Did you invite me over tonight just to give me the third degree?"

He was startled at the blunt question. "Uh, actually, it was Phoebe's idea to have you share a meal," he prevaricated.

"But I'm curious too," Phoebe chimed in. "What did you do out in the *Englisch* world?"

Adele glanced at Phoebe, and Isaiah saw her stance soften as he looked at the girl's face. "I did a lot of traveling," she said.

"Wow! Really? Where did you go?" asked Phoebe eagerly. Isaiah winced at the enthusiastic tone in her voice.

"All over," replied Adele, directing her answer to Phoebe. "I've been to Europe, Asia, Australia, the Caribbean, even South America."

Isaiah was interested despite himself. It wasn't often he met someone so well-traveled. "Were you a journalist or a correspondent that you traveled so widely?"

"*Nein.*" Her expression became neutral. "You—you might say I—I modeled."

With her beauty, that seemed a perfectly understandable explanation. No wonder she had traveled so much.

"It sounds so exotic," breathed Phoebe. Her eyes shone.

"It had its moments," admitted Adele. "But trust me when I say it's better here. I was never so happy to return to my roots."

"*Ja*, I agree," said Olivia with a certain forcefulness. "And Montana is some of the prettiest country I've seen. And the church here is so welcoming."

Isaiah got the distinct impression Olivia was diverting the conversation, but his curiosity about Adele ratcheted higher. He'd heard the modeling world could be ruthless and unforgiving. While he considered Adele to be the most beautiful woman he had ever seen, he doubted many women in their early thirties could make it in the merciless realm of modeling while competing with women much younger. "Why did you come back?" he asked, assuming she would confirm that theory.

"Because I realized the life I was living was shallow and…and heartless." She toyed with her glass of iced tea. "I left the Amish when I was eighteen and spent fifteen years doing what I thought was fulfilling. But it wasn't. Meanwhile, I realized how much Olivia had." She nodded at her sister. "A great *hutband*, a farm and…and a beautiful baby. I realized I had nothing. *Nothing.* It was then I realized I was far better off returning to the church with nothing, doing honest work and not selling my soul for things that no longer mattered."

It was about the longest speech he had gotten from her since making her acquaintance, and it spoke to a level of pain that had previously been untapped. He felt a little ashamed of himself for pushing.

Yet something didn't add up. Surely modeling was a lucrative line of work? If she had modeled since leaving the Amish at eighteen, why didn't she have any money saved up? Why did she have "nothing" after such a long career?

"I've always wanted to travel," said Phoebe, scooping some mashed potatoes onto her fork. "I had some *Englischer* friends back in Indiana that would go places every summer. Some went to Europe, a couple went to Australia and one friend spent a whole summer in Japan. It sounded so exciting! They showed me pictures too."

"I felt that way when I was your age," Adele said. "Like I would do anything to get away from the church. But trust me when I say it can get old. In my mind, there is nothing finer than what you've got here—developing a skill that can support you and being surrounded by a solid group of people who love you for who you are, not..." Her voice trailed off.

Isaiah was startled as her sentence remained unfinished. Was she going to say "not for what you look like"? He thought that might be it. After all, models weren't appreciated for their minds; they were wanted only because of their beautiful faces and bodies. He supposed being objectified like that would get old and unpleasant. No wonder she seemed cynical.

Yet wasn't that what he was doing—becoming attracted to Adele because of her beautiful face? It was an uncomfortable question he wasn't sure he wanted to ask himself.

He tuned back into the conversation as Phoebe demanded, "What was your favorite place you visited?"

Adele thought a moment. "Venice was beautiful, with its canals and old buildings, but it was very, very crowded. The view from the top of the Eiffel Tower was stunning, especially at night when the city was lit up. New Zealand was gorgeous—most of it is very wild and beautiful. Hong Kong was intense—very crowded, but very exciting. Tahiti had the most incredible beaches I've ever seen—crystal clear water, white sand, mountains covered with tropical vegetation."

Isaiah wasn't sure he liked this turn of conversation. One glance at his daughter confirmed she was hanging on every word. "Do you ever want to go back?" Phoebe asked.

"Nein." Adele spoke the word firmly. "Those locations are in my memory, but you know what's truly beautiful?"

"*Nein*, what?" Phoebe replied.

"This." She gestured toward the living room softly lit

up with oil lamps, the braided wool rug on the floor, then the kitchen table covered with homemade food. "When you've spent as many years as I have in nothing but luxurious surroundings, being served by people who are paid to serve you, you come to appreciate things that are plain and simple. I'm more impressed by your crafting skills and culinary ability than I can even say," she added on a serious note to Phoebe. "I never learned those things, and in some ways I feel like I'm just starting out, even though I'm thirty-three."

"Oh." Somewhat chastened, Phoebe toyed with her fork. She shrugged with an element of defensiveness. "It just seems old hat to me."

"It does until you're far away from it. Then it becomes something that beckons and calls. Don't give it up," Adele finished in a warning tone.

"That's easy for you to say," Phoebe argued back. "You had all those years to enjoy seeing the world. I haven't, but I want to."

"Phoebe…" Isaiah cautioned.

"*Nein*, it's true." His daughter looked stubborn. "I want to see these things too."

He met Adele's eyes over the table and saw regret in them. "I've said too much," she murmured.

He could hardly blame her, since he was the one that brought up the subject of her past to begin with. "It's nothing new," he said, and heard the weariness in his voice. "She's been saying that for some time."

"Stop talking as if I'm not here," Phoebe snapped. Then she looked horrified and glanced at Adele. "I'm sorry…"

To Isaiah's surprise, Adele chuckled. "You're so much like me at your age," she said. "I wanted nothing more than to leave. I couldn't wait to get out."

"Do you regret leaving?" Phoebe asked curiously.

"*Ja*." The single word came out with deep emotion. "More than I've ever regretted anything in my life. When I think how different my path might have been…"

Isaiah glanced at his daughter. She wore an almost comical expression of horror and defiance. "Well, I can't see how bad it could be, since you got to see all those beautiful places."

"There's beauty here, *liebling*," Adele replied softly. "More than you'll ever know."

Andrew, who had been largely silent, picked up his glass of iced tea and took a sip. "Tell me about the property," he prompted Isaiah. "You said it's twelve acres, *ja*?"

Isaiah grasped at the subject change with gratitude. "*Ja*, twelve. Enough for a cow or two…" And he dove into his plans for the farm.

Baby Helen started to fuss, so Olivia withdrew the baby from the bouncy seat in the center of the table and settled down to give the infant a bottle at the dinner table. Isaiah noticed the softness on Adele's face as she watched the tableau of mother and child.

Through the rest of the evening—beyond dinner, clean-up and lingering over conversation in the living room afterward—he noted how Olivia and Andrew asked many questions about neutral topics, both seeming to work at keeping the topic off Adele's past. With Olivia, he thought he saw a subtle air of protection concerning her sister.

Though he enjoyed the Eichers' company, the celebratory meal left Isaiah uncertain. He honestly didn't know whether to continue encouraging the friendship between Adele and his daughter. Nor was he really in a position to stop it, especially since they were now neighbors.

But the very fact that Adele had such broad travel experience in her past might lure his rebellious teen down a path he didn't want. Phoebe was at such an impulsive age that she might only hear the good parts of Adele's story and disregard the bad.

He was also in a quandary. He had admitted to the bishop that Adele was someone he might be interested in courting. Would inviting Adele further into Phoebe's life at this vulnerable junction be a benefit…or a detriment?

Chapter Twelve

In the week after Thanksgiving, Adele was inclined to beat herself up for sharing too much and dipping a little too close to the truth about her past. She wasn't sure where her impulsive claim of "modeling" came from, but it seemed to satisfy Isaiah's curiosity…to an extent. But it was a lie. And that lie, she knew, was likely to backfire on her someday.

She was disturbed by her own growing interest in Isaiah. She knew her path toward baptism depended on avoiding not just him, but all men.

Yet for how long? Even Olivia had admitted that it was unrealistic to expect this restriction to last the rest of her life. Should she wait until she was baptized before she confessed her interest? Or was she expected to remain single for the next few decades, becoming the proverbial lonely cat lady while watching her own daughter being raised by her sister?

The first week in December was busy at Yoder's Mercantile. Abe and Mabel and their employees festooned the store with cheerful but subdued Christmas decorations, and the townspeople packed the emporium, purchasing quilts and soaps and other Amish-made goods. Phoebe received three orders for rugs in the first week alone, to be delivered sometime during the new year.

The bakery and canning departments positively hummed as customers snapped up nearly everything they could churn out. Adele and Isaiah produced dozens of eggnog Bundt cakes and yule logs each week, on top of their regular cadre of goods.

By Saturday, she welcomed a day off. The weather had taken an unexpected warm swing, and she was able to sit in the rocking chair on the front porch, watching the kittens playing in the yard.

She'd thought of Phoebe a lot during the busy week of work, a week when Isaiah was courteous but more withdrawn. She couldn't blame him. She had a feeling he had concluded she was a bad influence on his daughter. It was a shame, too, because she had enjoyed Thanksgiving dinner with the two families, hers and Isaiah's.

Sitting in the rocking chair, she leafed through the only reminder she'd kept of her decade and a half of poor behavior—a thick photo album documenting many of the places she'd visited.

It was a dangerous item to possess since it was clear evidence of her life of scandal. She flipped through the pages, recalling the exciting places she'd been, when her only purpose was to be arm candy.

She looked at a photo of herself on the beach in Tahiti. She shuddered and turned the page to safer images of a sunset that didn't feature her.

Isaiah might see her pretty face, yes, but instinct told Adele his interest went deeper. Adele felt the same way toward him. Yet just the merest glimpse of her past was enough to cause him to pull back somewhat, at least where Phoebe was concerned.

The facade of domesticity around Thanksgiving continued to haunt her. She wanted a family. She *longed* for a family. But she had cut off that option when she embarked on her scandalous choices. Helen's father hadn't stuck around long enough even to know he had a daughter. At the time she gave up Helen to her sister, Adele hadn't thought she was cut out for motherhood.

What a sinful, mixed-up mess she was. Adele slapped the photo album closed and put it on the small side table next to the porch rocker. She leaned her head back and stared at the underside of the porch roof above her, thinking with envy about her sister's happy domestic situation. Maybe she should just get rid of that photo album altogether. It did nothing but remind her of days she wanted to forget…

"Adele!"

She raised her head and saw Phoebe trotting down the road toward her cabin. All her previous recriminating thoughts fled as she felt a flush of warmth and, yes, relief. Warmth because she was growing truly fond of the youngie, and relief to be diverted from her grim memories and self-loathing.

"*Guten tag!*" she called, rising to her feet.

"I've finished your carpets!" Phoebe called excitedly from the length of the driveway. "Would now be a *gut* time to bring them over? They're heavy, but *Daed* said he can load them in the wagon and drive them over."

"*Ja* sure!" she said with enthusiasm. "I'd love that!"

"Be back in a few minutes, then!" Phoebe trotted back toward the farm and disappeared behind a screen of shrubbery.

Adele jumped up and dashed into the house, surveying it with a critical eye. She hastily made her bed, washed a few dishes, and gave the cabin a quick tidying.

She was still sweeping the floor when she heard the rumble of a wagon and the clip-clop of hooves. She stepped out onto the porch and saw Isaiah guiding the horse down the brief stretch of road between their driveways, with Phoebe on the seat beside him. Was it wrong that her heart gave a little leap of excitement at the sight of him?

But she composed her features, smoothed down her apron and went out to meet them.

"I hope you like them!" called Phoebe. The moment the wagon stopped, she jumped down from the seat and went around to the back, where the rolled-up carpets were tied with twine.

"They're heavy," warned Isaiah, putting the brake on the wagon and the reins in the holder before climbing down from the seat. "Phoebe and I can carry in the larger rug. I can come back for the smaller one."

"I can probably carry the smaller one myself," she offered. She went to the back of the wagon and saw the earth-toned rugs gleaming in the afternoon sunshine. "Oh Phoebe, they look beautiful."

"Wait until you see them spread out," the youngie said. "Okay, *Daed*, ready?"

Together, father and daughter hoisted the larger rolled-up rug on their shoulders and headed for the house. Not to be outdone, Adele pulled the smaller carpet out of the wagon, balanced the bundle on her shoulder and plodded after them.

Inside the cabin, Isaiah and Phoebe laid the larger carpet in the center of the living room floor. Adele deposited the smaller carpet out of the way as Isaiah pulled out a pocket knife and sliced open the cordage. He and Phoebe proceeded to unroll the carpet and drag it into position in the center of the room.

"Oooohh," breathed Adele. "It's stunning!"

It was indeed. The heavy wool fabric absorbed some

of the sound in the room and instantly made the living space feel cozier and more domestic. The primary color was brown, heavily interspersed with red and forest green and just a touch of dark blue, like bits of gems or colored leaves on a forest floor. Some of the fabrics were striped, some were herringbone, some were plaid, and all added to the overall glory of the finished product.

Impulsively Adele reached out and pulled Phoebe into a hug. "I'm so pleased!" she exclaimed. "It's the most beautiful rug I've ever seen!"

She felt the warmth of the girl's body as the youngie hugged her back, and a wave of maternal affection washed over her such as she'd never felt except lately, when holding Helen. But Phoebe was nearly grown, and the emotion was different than when holding her baby—pride and friendship, and maybe a bit of love.

The two drew apart, and Adele was surprised to see a sparkle of moisture in the teen's eyes.

"Well." Phoebe turned away. "I hope you'll like your smaller rug too. Is it going in the bedroom?"

"*Ja*, right next to the bed, so I have something warm for my bare feet when I get up."

Isaiah hefted the rolled up rug onto his shoulder, and Adele—suddenly feeling awkward—led the way into the bedroom. He sliced the twine and rolled out the floor covering, and Adele slid it into position to her satisfaction.

"All the difference in the world," Adele announced. The bedroom rug, about three by five feet, was a smaller version of the larger one in the living room and created a similar impression of warmth and coziness. "And now," she added with a grin, "for the best part. Follow me."

Adele led the way back into the kitchen, where she pulled a small envelope from a drawer. Inside was cash she had pulled out of her paychecks to pay for the carpets. With great ceremony, she counted out the bills until she reached the total amount due, then added some more for a tip. "Because they're so beautiful, and I want to encourage you to continue," she said.

"*Danke*," breathed Phoebe, staring at the pile of money. She seemed afraid to pick it up, so Adele did it for her. She tucked the currency back into the envelope and handed it over to the teen.

"*Danke*," Phoebe repeated, grinning and clutching the envelope to her chest. "I almost feel guilty accepting it."

"Don't," replied Adele. "You've earned it. And just look at the difference those rugs make." She gestured toward the living room. "Honestly, I'm looking forward to taking off my shoes and stockings and walking across them barefoot. Now that winter's here and I have the woodstove going almost all the time, those rugs will make a world of difference in comfort."

"And they'll last you a lifetime," Phoebe added. "Wool rag rugs will last fifty years or more."

"That's why you shouldn't feel guilty for accepting payment," concluded Adele. "I consider it an investment—not just in home furnishings, but in your talent. Can you stay for tea?" she added.

"*Ja* sure!" The teen grinned.

Isaiah hesitated, then capitulated. "I'll be going. I have some work to do this afternoon."

"*Vielen dank* for driving them over," she told him.

He touched the brim of his hat and left. After a few moments, she heard him cluck to his horse and then the crunch of gravel under hooves and wheels.

"So how many carpets are you working on now?" Adele

asked, guiding Phoebe toward the kitchen. "I understand you got some orders from the *Englischer* in town, *ja*?"

As she made tea, she wondered how she could direct the conversation around to the issue of the teen's desire to leave the church. But it wasn't something to be hurried.

Instead she listened as Phoebe described her position as the fiber-arts ambassador for Yoder's Mercantile, the experience of meeting and talking to some of the women in the settlement and her plans for the three carpet orders she had received in the post-Thanksgiving, pre-Christmas rush in the store.

"I've heard nothing but praise from the Yoders for what you're doing," Adele said toward the end of the recital. "It sounds like you could have a job for life."

"Maybe." Phoebe traced the edge of her mug with a thumb. "I just don't know if it's what I want to do. I keep thinking of all the travel adventures you've had, and I… I…"

"Don't forget," Adele said gently. "I'm happiest here. I missed so much by leaving when I wasn't much older than you. I gave up so much."

"I know." Phoebe's shoulders slumped. "And yet I haven't found any reason to stay. Instead, I want to be just like you."

Just like you. The words chilled Adele, yet she could hardly tell the youngie the true horrors of what she'd lived through.

Long after Phoebe thanked her and went home, Adele wondered what kind of influence she was having on the girl…and if she should stop seeing her.

Isaiah couldn't figure out whether to be pleased or alarmed by his daughter's behavior in the aftermath of delivering the rugs.

For days after, Phoebe seemed more cheerful, and she talked about Adele incessantly. "I want to be just like her," the girl said more than once.

Isaiah couldn't fault his daughter for neglecting either her household chores or her work on behalf of the Yoders. She was diligent in working on her craft, and she was collaborating closely with Mabel Yoder on the creation of the new fiber-arts section of the store. But over the next week, Phoebe looked for any and every opportunity to talk to Adele, either in the store or by walking over to see her.

He supposed it was normal for the teen to develop a sort of hero-worship for a woman who had seen so much and traveled to so many exotic destinations. And Adele, to her credit, made no effort to encourage Phoebe to want to see those things herself, repeating that she was happier where she currently was.

What alarmed Isaiah was that the restlessness that had plagued Phoebe before moving here to Montana—a restlessness cultivated by her association with *Englischer* friends—seemed to be returning. And as before, he didn't know how to stop it. It wasn't like he could move again to a different state solely to keep Phoebe sheltered.

And he had to accept reality. If Phoebe was not inclined to become a baptized member of the church, he could hardly force her…though his heart broke at the thought of losing her to the *Englisch* world.

But at some level, Phoebe's obsession with Adele was starting to disturb him, and he couldn't pinpoint why—especially since he, too, was obsessed with Adele, for a different reason.

Adele had become more talkative since their Thanksgiving dinner and later the rug delivery. At work, she chatted with him more comfortably about everyday things, and he avoided dredging up anything that might remind her of what appeared to be a painful past.

"I can't wait to get cows again," he remarked, dropping raw bagels into boiling water. "I'm getting two Jerseys from Ephraim King next week, so Phoebe and I have been working on the fencing and fixing up the barn to get ready for them. They both should be calving within a few months, so I'll be milking again. I like milking."

"I used to hate it," she admitted. "But then I hated a lot of things when I was a youngie. I've changed my perspective on so many things. I wonder if milking is one of them."

"You're renting now," he asked. "But what do you want in the future? Do you want a place of your own? Do you want a farm?"

"I doubt I could ever afford a place of my own," she replied. "I'm starting out with nothing."

Once again he longed to ask her why, after a long career of modeling, she had no material assets to show for it. There was something peculiar here, something he didn't understand. But he could hardly grill her on something so personal.

"Well, I don't mind the milking routine, especially since I only milk once a day," he said. "I separate the calves at night and just milk in the morning, so that frees me from a lot of hassle, especially since I have a day job. It's not like I'm a dairy farmer."

"What do you do with the milk?"

"Make cheese, mostly. Cheddar is our favorite, and sometimes I make mozzarella or cream cheese, but usually only when I want to make pizza or cheesecake or something specific."

"Will you sell your cheese here in the store?"

"*Nein*. Abe Yoder told me most of the cheese they sell

comes from Aaron Lapp, who lives in the settlement. I'm sure you've met him—he's hard to miss since his face is heavily scarred from getting caught in a barn fire many years ago."

"*Ja,* I've met him. Nice man. I didn't know he made cheese, though."

"Apparently he's the best cheesemaker in the settlement, and makes all kinds. Swiss, Gouda, cheddar, parmesan, that kind of thing."

"Impressive."

They both worked in silence for a few minutes. He boiled bagels. She braided Christmas sweetbreads.

"I miss having chickens," she remarked at last, her eyes on her work. "That's one farm chore I enjoyed as a youngie. Even when I was older, I felt there was something magical about gathering eggs. I don't think Eli Miller—he's my landlord—would want me to get chickens though."

"We just got chickens," he said. "It's too late in the year for chicks, but Ephraim sold me five laying hens. It's nice to have fresh eggs again."

"*Ja.*" She gave a little sigh. "I'll just have to be patient."

Maybe not for long, he thought to himself. If she agreed to let him court her at some future point, he would guarantee her all the chickens she wanted, of whatever breeds her heart desired.

As he and Phoebe settled into their new farm, he found he was developing it with Adele in mind.

In the years after his wife's untimely death, he had been reeling from grief, caught up in raising his child in the absence of her mother and trying to make a living at the same time.

But his wife had been gone for seven years now. He

could begin thinking about courting again. And Adele was single…

But was she a bad influence on his daughter? He didn't know.

Phoebe entered the bakery. "I'm finished for the day," she told him. "When you have a chance, go out into the main part of the store and look at the display Mabel and I put together. It shows the miniature rugs I made, along with a small section of an unsewn braided strip."

"I'm in the middle of a task," he told her. "But I'll look as soon as I can."

"I can take a moment." Adele dusted off her hands. "I'm anxious to see it."

"*Ja gut!*" Phoebe smiled with enthusiasm. "And Mabel says it's just the beginning!"

Isaiah watched the two disappear into the main part of the store. Adele was always like that—encouraging his daughter in her skills. He blessed Mabel Yoder, too, for cultivating his daughter's talent.

But was it enough to keep his only child from fleeing the church? He didn't know.

Later that evening, as he and Phoebe did some fence repair on the farm in anticipation of getting the cows, he asked, "What did Adele think of your display in the store?"

"She loved it." Phoebe pulled off her canvas work gloves and used her bare fingers to expertly wrap wire to hold the field fence to a T-post. "She also told me again how much she loves the carpets I made her." She was silent a moment, then added, "I like Adele."

Isaiah decided to delve into unknown territory—unknown and just a bit frightening. But if he and Adele had any possibility of a future together, it would have to be with the blessing of his daughter, who remained his top priority.

He snipped some wire and proceeded to attach another piece of fence to the next T-post. "How would you feel if I were to court Adele?" he asked, then held his breath for the answer.

Phoebe turned a surprised face to him, then a smile lit her face. "That would be *wunnerschee*!" she exclaimed. "I would like to have her for a mother. Well, stepmother."

His breath whooshed out in relief, and he smiled back. "I've already mentioned the possibility of courting her to the bishop," he admitted. "But since she's not baptized, he did advise me to take things slow. If she's open to being courted, I doubt we could get married for at least a year, maybe two. Whatever happens, don't mention it to her. Don't breathe a word to anyone. I have to trust you on that point, Phoebe."

"I won't say anything. I promise." Phoebe returned to her work, a smile still on her face. "I wonder why she never had any children?" she mused. "And how she would like me as a daughter."

"I don't see how she could help liking you as a daughter," he answered. He was warmed by Phoebe's approval. It was the first step toward courting Adele—and the most important one.

"I think we're about done here," he said at last, looking down the line of tidy fencing. "I have a bit more work to do in the barn before the cows arrive, but that can wait until tomorrow. Plus it will be dark soon, and I'm getting hungry. Let's go make some dinner."

They gathered their tools and gloves and trudged back toward the farmhouse, dumping their gear on the back porch.

"Don't forget to take care of the chickens," he reminded her. "I'll start dinner while you're doing that. Lentils and onions?" he added, referring to a fast and filling spicy dish they both enjoyed.

"*Ja* sure," she said. "I won't be long." She headed off into the gloom toward the coop, where the five ladies now resided.

Isaiah went inside and went to pluck some onions from a bin when he realized he was still carrying Phoebe's work gloves. He went to put them in her bedroom.

He had just dropped the gloves on her bed when his eye was caught by something completely out of place in an Amish home: a photo album, resting on the seat of the rocking chair in the corner of the room.

A photo album? Where on earth had his daughter gotten something as foreign as a photo album?

Curious, he opened the volume…and his world shattered.

Chapter Thirteen

Adele lit an oil lamp against the dusk of the evening and placed it on the kitchen table, then added a piece of firewood to the wood cookstove. The early December air outside was chilly, and she wondered how long they had before the first snow fell. But here in the cabin, the warmth felt good. The kittens seemed to think so too, for they both lounged on Phoebe's beautiful wool carpet, as close to the stove as they could get without leaving the sanctuary of the rug.

Adele sat down at the table and tried to think of what kinds of gifts she could give Isaiah and Phoebe for Christmas.

The trouble was, she had no skills or talents. Her sister Olivia was a skilled basketmaker. Other women could knit, crochet, sew, make quilts and engage in endless other crafts. Phoebe had a wonderful skill with her rugs.

But as for herself? Nothing. She had been too busy cultivating her looks when she was Phoebe's age, rather than cultivating any other talents. Now that dearth weighed on her heavily, especially when she wanted to gift something to Isaiah and Phoebe.

It made her wonder if she was cut out for marriage. Honestly, what did she have to offer in a relationship? If Isaiah was ever inclined to court her, what would she bring to the partnership except her beautiful face? She knew by now it wasn't enough.

She had been away for so long, and so many skills she had brushed off as unnecessary when she was a youngie now seemed desirable. Well, she could learn them now, but she would be starting from scratch. She had nothing to show for fifteen years away from her roots except a photo album she was tempted to throw away so as not to be reminded of her painful past.

She forced her mind away from previous regrets to consider her current problem of Christmas gifts. She wanted to do something—anything—to show her growing affection for Phoebe and, yes, for Isaiah too.

Baking something was out of the question. There was nothing she could bake that Isaiah couldn't bake better.

So what could she offer as a gift? Unless…

She resisted the urge to clunk herself upside the head. She could embroider something. It was the one modest skill she had.

Encouraged, she fetched a sheet of paper and a pencil and started sketching ideas. Perhaps she could make a snow scene with pine trees and a bright cardinal for Isaiah. For Phoebe, she thought about a wreath decorated with pinecones and ornaments, with a small deer in the center. Phoebe liked deer.

An embroidered ornament seemed appropriate somehow. A gift of the heart, but nothing too personal or too obvious.

Absorbed in the sketches and pleased with her initial ideas, she nearly jumped out of her skin when a sudden knock sounded on the door. The kittens were equally startled, and scattered from their spot on the carpet.

Wary, she padded toward the door. "Who is it?"

"Isaiah. And Phoebe."

Startled, she unlocked the door and swung it wide open with a smile. "*Gut'n owed! Komm* in!"

Her smile faded when she saw a look of furious anger on Isaiah's face. Behind him, Phoebe stood silently, her eyes red-rimmed. He did not enter the house but remained on the porch. Confused, Adele looked from one to the other. "What's wrong?"

"I moved here," he snapped, "leaving behind friends and family, solely to save my daughter from being persuaded by outsiders to leave the faith. For a while I thought it worked. But now…now I find out you've been undermining my efforts. I want to know why you've been trying to turn Phoebe away from her roots and toward the *Englisch* world."

Adele was honestly bewildered. "What are you talking about? I haven't done anything to sway Phoebe away from the faith."

"You're wrong. You've been filling her head with exotic destinations and faraway places, and now she tells me she doesn't want to get baptized at all."

Adele shifted her gaze to Phoebe, still hovering in the background, her shoulders bowed. "Phoebe?" Adele's voice was gentle. "What's this all about?"

A stubborn silence descended on the porch. Phoebe kept her eyes on the boards beneath her and refused to look up.

"Phoebe, I can't help if I don't know what's wrong," Adele tried again.

"Why are you pretending ignorance?" Isaiah said, his voice filled with gravel and wood chips. "You know what you've done, and I can't forgive it."

She met his eyes. "No, Isaiah. I don't know what I've done. Why don't you tell me?"

"I already did. The traveling you've done before returning here—can you tell me a youngie like Phoebe isn't going to want to do the same thing? Why would you support that?"

"I haven't supported that." She wanted to shout her defense, but kept her voice level. She could hear the suppressed anger in her tone and raised her chin to look him square in the eye. "I think I made it perfectly clear those days are behind me and I want nothing more to do with them."

"Then why have you continued encouraging it?" Isaiah growled. "You leave me no option, Adele. You are forbidden from seeing my daughter again."

She heard a tiny gasp from Phoebe. Furiously, Adele drew herself up. "How dare you trespass in my home and speak to me in this manner?" she spat. "*Ja*, you have the ability to keep Phoebe away from me, though you're doing your daughter a disservice if you think that's going to change her mind about getting baptized. But you have no right to accuse me of something I didn't do or accost me in such a manner…especially when you refuse to tell me what's happening."

She was gratified to see shock on his face, as if he didn't expect to be reprimanded for his behavior. Drawing on her success, she said, "Good night, Isaiah. Unfortunately I have no option but to work with you at the bakery, but rest assured, this won't be forgotten."

She slammed the door, her heart beating fast. She waited a few moments then peered out the window. She could make out Isaiah trudging away in the late dusk, with Phoebe trailing behind him, her feet dragging. The girl's shoulders shook as though she was weeping. Adele's heart went out to the girl.

Whatever the provocation, it seemed Phoebe's secret was out. Isaiah now knew his daughter was resisting the notion of being baptized. Adele prayed the youngie would not follow the path she, herself, had taken.

More than her concern over Phoebe, Adele was hurt and baffled by the confrontation. Feeling overheated, she went outside and sat down in the rocking chair on the front porch, watching the dusk deepening into night. She wanted to weep with vexation. What just happened?

Just minutes ago, her mind was pleasantly filled with the notion of Christmas presents. Now she wanted to throw something in a fit of pique.

What on earth had Isaiah meant about filling Phoebe's head with exotic destinations and faraway places? Was he referring to the conversation over Thanksgiving dinner, when Phoebe had asked where she had traveled? She had made it clear she preferred it here.

The confrontation made her realize how deeply in love she had fallen with Isaiah. The sense of friendship and security she'd found with him was more precious than the jewelry she'd once owned in abundance. And now it was gone…

She huffed out a breath of frustration, staring out at the darkening landscape. In the span of just a few minutes, she had not only lost the budding mentorship with a youngie she hoped to keep in the church, but somehow she had also lost the man she had dreamed about a future relationship with…and she had no idea why.

Something nagged at her, something about sitting in this rocking chair on the porch. Something to do with Isaiah and Phoebe. She had never sat on the porch with them, so why was she thinking she had?

Suddenly she realized the last time she'd sat in this chair, she had been despairing over the photos contained in her album. She had left the album…on the table next to the rocking chair.

She felt the blood drain from her face. The table was empty. She jumped to her feet and searched around the porch, but found nothing. She went inside, picked up the oil lamp for extra light and searched the entire porch. The album was gone.

It wasn't hard to put two and two together and realize Phoebe must have taken the album. That meant the youngie had seen pictures of all the exotic locations she'd visited. Adele's face burned with humiliation when she realized she was in most of those photos, often with the men she was dating at the time.

Had Isaiah seen those pictures? Was that why he'd accused her of influencing Phoebe away from the church? Did he think she'd given the album to the teen? Why, oh, why hadn't she gotten rid of the album before this?

Now he was furious at her, blaming her for Phoebe's refusal to be baptized. The unfairness of the situation galled her. Phoebe's issues long preceded Isaiah's arrival in Montana—he'd said as much. Why was Isaiah focusing on her background, when it was clear Phoebe's reluctance to remain Amish was far beyond Adele's influence?

She couldn't let this go. She had dreamed about a future with Isaiah and Phoebe. If that dream had any chance of becoming a reality, then they needed to know about her past. And maybe—she prayed—her experiences might sway Phoebe away from repeating her own mistakes.

With determined steps, she descended the porch stairs and walked over to Isaiah's farm.

Once Isaiah and Phoebe got home, his daughter immediately ran into her bedroom and slammed the door. He stared at the barrier and sighed.

His daughter was slipping away from his grasp, and he felt powerless to do anything about it. Perhaps banning Adele from seeing her was not the wisest thing to do, but seldom had he felt such fury as he had when leafing through the pages of the photo album and seeing Adele posing in endless stunning locations, each more beautiful than the last. How could Phoebe resist such temptation?

Isaiah was concerned for another reason. Surrounded by women wearing Plain clothing, it disturbed him to see photos of Adele in *Englisch* attire—not just the occasional bikini photo, but in slinky dresses and casual shorts and other apparel. While this was understandable if she had worked as a model, he hadn't really connected the reality of what modeling entailed to the shy and modest woman he'd known for the last two months.

His stomach clenched at the thought of Phoebe wearing that kind of clothing. But if she left the church and made her way in the *Englisch* world, she would blend in better in that clothing than if she wore her apron and *kapp*. It was all so complicated…

Suddenly he heard a knock at the door. He frowned. He wasn't in the mood for visitors, not after the last hour.

He approached the door. "Who is it?"

"Adele. Let me in, Isaiah. We need to talk."

He whisked open the door, knowing his face looked like a thundercloud. "I'm not in the mood right now, Adele."

"*Ja*, well, neither am I. But I have something to say to both you and Phoebe, and you'd better listen."

The grim certainty in her voice pierced his resentment. He stared at her for a moment, then stepped aside so she could enter. The house was lit with oil lamps, and he could see the no-nonsense expression on her face—and something more. Defiance. She looked defiant.

"Isaiah, I know you're upset about Phoebe. But you can't prevent her from leaving, and the harder you try, the more determined she'll be. Take it from me. If she doesn't want to be baptized, you can't force her. That's the whole purpose behind adult baptism—so individuals can decide for themselves whether this is the life they want."

"Is that why you're here?" he snapped. "To continue undermining my attempts to keep her in the church?"

"*Nein*. I'm here to do the opposite. I have something I need to tell both you and Phoebe. Especially Phoebe. It may help."

He examined her face. It was drawn and tight, as though she was dreading something. He made a sudden decision.

"Let me get Phoebe," he said. He went over and knocked on his daughter's bedroom door. "Phoebe? Adele is here. She has something to say to us both."

Without waiting for a response, he went back into the living room. Within a few moments, Phoebe followed, looking sulky and resentful.

Adele addressed Phoebe. "*Leibling*, did you take my photo album?"

Take? Isaiah stared at Adele. He thought she'd *given* the album to his daughter.

"*Ja*," muttered Phoebe.

"Why?"

"Because…because I saw the first page, that picture of you on the beach in Tahiti, and I wanted to see more. But I had a feeling you wouldn't want me to." The teen twisted a corner of her apron.

"Well, you're right. I wouldn't have wanted you to. Phoebe, you told me some time ago you don't want to be baptized. Now your father says the same thing. Why?"

"Because I want something different!" the girl burst out.

"I want to do what you did, seeing the world and all those beautiful places. Someday I'd like to have a photo album with similar photos, but with myself in them."

Isaiah felt a thrill of horror at his daughter's words. But Adele looked sad. "I think we should all sit down," she said quietly. "I have a story to tell, and it's not pretty."

Without waiting for acknowledgment, she went over and seated herself in a rocking chair. After a moment's pause, Isaiah followed. Phoebe sat opposite. There was a few moments' silence, punctuated only by the ticking of the clock over the kitchen sink at the far side of the room.

"I'm fond of you both," Adele began. "Fonder than I can say. And for that reason, I need to tell you what happened to me when I was just a little bit older than you, Phoebe. I was eighteen years old. I want you both to know before… before anything else happens. It's an ugly story, and I am resigned to the fact that both of you may hate me after you hear this."

Hate her? Isaiah was jolted out of his own misery. What was so bad that she felt they would hate her?

Now it was Adele's turn to twist a corner of her apron in agitation. The room was silent for a few moments while she appeared to gather her thoughts.

"I knew from an early age I didn't want to be baptized," she began. "Probably from age eleven or twelve. Part of that certainty arose around the time I realized I was b-beautiful." She paused for a moment, as if overcome, then continued. "You've seen my sister, Olivia. She can only charitably be described as plain. It's like *Gott* gave me all the beauty he took away from her. Yet it hardly needs to be said who ended up the more blessed sister."

Isaiah saw Adele glance at Phoebe, who was listening with rapt attention.

"My mother died when I was very young, just five years old," Adele continued. "Our father raised us both as best he knew how, and I know my teenage rebellion frustrated and confused him. He was a *gut* man, and to my dying day I will regret causing him such pain. At any rate, I left the church when I was eighteen to make my way in the *Englisch* world. I wanted to live in a city and experience all the glitter and glamor it represented."

She stopped and took a shuddering breath. "It wasn't easy," she continued. "I tried getting various jobs—at a department store, a coffee shop, a grocery store. Everywhere I went, I had attention from men because of my looks. I'll admit I enjoyed the attention, but the one thing I didn't enjoy was trying to make a living. Minimum wage jobs in large cities don't go far when there's rent to pay and food to buy. So—so I found an easier w-way."

Isaiah saw tears well in her eyes. She fished a handkerchief out of her pocket and mopped her face.

"I—I d-decided that my beauty was the key," she continued in a shaking voice. "And s-so I started dating wealthy men. Men who only wanted me for one reason."

Isaiah was shocked down to his core. This was the absolute last thing he expected. "I th-thought you said you were a model?" he stuttered.

"That was stretching the truth," she told him. She met his eyes, her own red-rimmed. "But I was desperate. I didn't know where to turn."

"What do you mean?" asked Phoebe in confusion.

How could he explain to his innocent daughter? He was groping around in his mind to try to find the right words, when Adele spoke first.

"*Liebling*, I dated wealthy men in exchange for…for favors. That's how I was able to see the world. I traded my virtue for pleasure seeking."

The youngie's jaw dropped as the full meaning of Adele's words sank in. The girl wore an expression of utter shock.

Adele nodded sadly. "And that's how I lived for fifteen years. When one man got tired of me, I found another. It was a soulless existence, but I didn't realize that for a long time. It seemed exciting to be wined and dined, to visit exotic places around the world, to wear beautiful and expensive clothing and jewelry. But a little over a year ago, I got pregnant."

Phoebe sucked in her breath. Even Isaiah braced himself for the worst. Surely she didn't...

"The man I was with had no interest in a b-baby," continued Adele in a shaking voice. "When I came back after giving birth in the hospital, I found I had been robbed. Cleaned out. Jewelry, cash, my credit cards...all taken. I'm certain it was done by the baby's father as a final slap in the face, though I couldn't prove it. But it left me virtually destitute. I never bothered saving money in the bank because I had always been taken care of."

She took a deep shuddering breath. "So I f-found another man as soon as I could. It was the only thing I knew how to do. But he didn't want to deal with a newborn, so I did the unthinkable. I abandoned my own b-baby to my sister."

Isaiah hadn't expected this. But he clearly remembered Olivia's husband Andrew telling him their baby was adopted...

Tears spilled silently down Adele's face. "A-and then the man I thought would be my next boyfriend after I had given my baby to Olivia dropped me for a younger model in Europe," she said. "That's when I c-came back to Olivia and begged for help. I knew by this point *Gott* wasn't happy with me. It j-just took me a long t-time to recognize it."

Isaiah glanced at Phoebe. Her hand was over her mouth, her eyes enormous as she stared at Adele in horror.

"I had to hit rock bottom before I could admit how wrong I was to leave the church," Adele said with a sob. "I was destitute. My own sister was raising the baby I'd abandoned. My life was so *ugly*, despite my beauty. It's not all glitter and glamor out there in the *Englisch* world. I saw many wonderful things, but I had to debase myself to see them. That is the reality of what happens by leading a sinful life." She looked at Phoebe through her tears. "*Liebling*, I don't want the same thing to happen to you. You have no idea how much support you'll be giving up if you leave the church—both materially and emotionally. I don't want you to reach my age with so many regrets that you come crawling back, begging *Gott*'s forgiveness as well as the forgiveness of your family. That's one of the things I've been trying to do—to guide you away from that idea."

Silence fell on the room except for the sound of Phoebe's harsh breathing. His daughter continued to look shocked and horrified. Suddenly she burst into tears, leaped to her feet and ran from the room. Isaiah winced at the sound of the slammed door.

Adele looked at him sadly. "This is why my sister—and the bishop—discouraged me from associating with men. Leaving my past behind is part of my redemption to join the church, something I desperately want to do. Isaiah, I was the worst kind of sinner anyone can imagine, and my life was hell. It's not anymore."

He honestly didn't know what to say.

After a few moments of silence, she rose to her feet,

moving like an old woman. She looked at him gravely. "I'm sorry, Isaiah," she whispered.

Before he could stop her, she too had fled, disappearing out the front door into the night.

Chapter Fourteen

Adele didn't sleep that night. Every time she tried lying down, visions of the evening's drama flooded her brain and propelled her back out of bed to engage in frantic, useless activities around the cabin—scouring the kitchen sink, sweeping the floor, even playing with the kittens, despite the animals' obvious desire to sleep.

Isaiah's disgust at her confession made her realize how much she yearned for Isaiah's love. Instead, now he was understandably repulsed by her, and she couldn't blame him. But it left her even more destitute—emotionally—than when she'd been abandoned by Helen's father after the baby's birth. This emotional upheaval was far more painful that she could imagine.

Finally, in an effort to calm her unsettled mind, she pulled out her embroidery supplies and began transferring her sketches to cloth. It seemed strange and perhaps foolish to be embroidering at three o'clock in the morning, but it was better than tossing and turning in bed.

The oil lamp purred on the table. The kittens curled up on the wool rug. The wood in the woodstove gave small crackles as it burned. Adele threaded a needle and began to outline the scene she had sketched.

The activity was soothing, but unfortunately it still left

her brain free to fret and worry. She couldn't shake the thought that she had utterly ruined her chances of becoming baptized. And if that was the case, what then? Would she lose her job, her rental home, her church connections? What could she do? Where could she go?

When dawn finally broke, she realized the embroidered ornament was shaping up nicely. With the growing daylight, common sense returned. Just because Isaiah and Phoebe knew about her past, it did not jeopardize her path to redemption. She had the backing of the bishop, who already knew the truth of what she had done. All it did, in fact, was jeopardize her standing with Phoebe—and Isaiah. And that, more than almost anything else, worried her.

She rose from the kitchen chair, stiff from sitting for many hours, and stretched before starting a kettle on the stove for tea. She splashed some water on her face and was glad it was Saturday and she could avoid seeing Isaiah until Monday. Tomorrow was an "off Sunday" as well, so there was no church. She could sulk in silence.

She sipped her tea while sitting outside on the porch in the cold morning air. She was tired after her sleepless night, yes, but more than that, she was depressed. She had sacrificed her future by confessing her past.

She wished she hadn't been banned by Andrew from visiting her sister's farm because she could use some advice from Olivia at the moment. Her younger sister had always been the hard-headed, practical one, and Adele realized just how much she depended on Olivia's good judgment. Surely she would know how to handle the situation.

Adele abruptly decided to risk his wrath in an effort to see her sister. If they had a telephone, she would call. In the absence of that option, she had little choice but to trespass.

It was far too early, barely dawn, so Adele knew she

had to wait for a more reasonable hour. She brought her cooling tea indoors, restoked the fire and went back to her embroidery.

Around nine o'clock, she donned a cloak against the chilly air and set out toward Olivia and Andrew's farm. The gravel roads on the settlement were deserted. The silence seemed ominous to Adele's overstretched mind, but the lack of buggies or pedestrians was surely just coincidental.

Sunk in her misery, she found her way to the farm faster than she would have thought. A cheerful puff of smoke made the picturesque home seem impossibly cozy. Adele stood for a moment on the walkway below the porch then took a deep breath and climbed the porch steps. Her knock sounded loud in the frosty air.

She heard footsteps, and the door whisked open. Andrew stood there and gaped in surprise. "Adele!"

"I'm sorry to trespass," she said hurriedly, forestalling the expected order to go away. "But I need to talk to Olivia. If you could ask her to meet me at my cabin, I'd be grateful." She turned and walked back down the porch steps.

She was halfway down the walkway when she heard Andrew call, "Adele, wait. If you came all this way just to speak to Olivia, I can't say no. Come inside."

She turned, her cloak tugged closely around her, and soberly regarded her brother-in-law. He gave her a small smile, and she realized in that instant that he had forgiven her earlier transgressions. It lightened her dark mood.

"*Veilen dank*, Andrew," she said in all seriousness. "I promise you I will never, ever breach your trust again."

"You've proven to be a woman of your word," he replied. "Would you like some tea?"

"*Ja, bitte*. I haven't slept all night, so any extra caffeine would be welcome."

Andrew stepped aside as she climbed the porch steps once again, and she went inside the cabin. Instantly she was besieged by the same envy she'd felt before at her sister's happiness. Her daughter, Helen, sat in a bouncy seat on the table, gumming a teething ring, and Olivia was stirring something on the stove.

"Adele!" she exclaimed. She dropped her wooden spoon and embraced her. "This is a surprise!" She shot a quick look at her husband, who shrugged.

"Andrew said I could come in. I n-needed to talk to you…" To Adele's annoyance, she began tearing up.

"Ach, sit down, *liebling*."

Adele collapsed at the table and to her annoyance, burst into tears.

Olivia let her cry for a few minutes while Andrew busied himself making tea. By the time he set a steaming mug in front of her, the storm had passed and Adele was mopping her face with a handkerchief. "I'm sorry…" she began.

Olivia waved a hand. "Obviously something happened. What is it?"

So Adele blurted out the whole wretched story, from the moment Isaiah showed up last night with Phoebe in tow to her sleepless night, worried now that her secret was out.

"And I d-don't know what to d-do." She hiccupped. She blew her nose then wrapped her hands around the hot ceramic of the mug of tea. "At first I was worried this whole thing might jeopardize my chances of getting baptized, but I realize now that's not likely to happen. The bishop has my back on that. But I… I…"

"But you're worried how this will affect your relationship with Isaiah," concluded Olivia with a crooked smile.

"*Ja*." Adele slumped at the table and stared at her mug,

not even responding when little Helen dropped her teething ring and let out a wail.

Andrew handed his daughter the toy. "Would it help if I spoke to him?"

"And say what?" Adele gave a small shake of her head. "I'm sorry, that was rude. But I told him the truth. What more can I say? I have no intention of trying to lure Phoebe away from the church. Just the opposite—I want to convince her it's far better to stay. But I could tell he was repulsed by my past, and I d-don't see how he could ever get over that. And now I have t-to work with him in the b-bakery..."

"*Liebling*, stop." Olivia's quiet voice cut through Adele's blather. "First of all, you need to give Isaiah a few days' time to calm down. I won't deny it was probably a shock to him, if he had plans to court you. Whether he can get over that shock is something no one knows, least of all him. But if he can't, he's not the man for you anyway."

"I know." Adele sniffed. "But it's the first time I've ever fallen in love with someone, and I find it's a raw and humiliating experience."

"Not always." Andrew shot a look at his wife filled with such love that Adele had to swallow hard. "Sorting things out may take time, but it's worth it. I have a feeling, Adele, that Isaiah may come around."

"What makes you say that?" She tried to deny the shaft of hope that went through her.

"If the woman at the well can be forgiven for her sins, why not you?" he countered, referencing the famous Bible story. "And the reason I suspect he may come around is because, as you said earlier, the bishop has your back. That's a powerful ally in your corner, and Isaiah would look foolish if he tried to hold your past over your head."

Adele slumped again. "He may forgive me, but he may not want to court me. And I wouldn't blame him. What man would want to be yoked to such damaged goods?"

"*Liebling*, when you first came back to us a few months ago, I said you had to first learn to love yourself," Olivia said gently. "I don't think you have."

"That's the thing," replied Adele. "Until a short while ago, I thought I had. I was feeling optimistic about the future. I'm making friends. I enjoy my work. I love going to church services. I guess I'm facing a new problem—dealing with the scorn of the first man whose good opinion I value. That's a new one for me."

"And it may not be the last." Olivia held out her hands across the table. "But come what may, Adele, you're loved for yourself. Speaking as your sister, I can't tell you how wonderful it is to have you back. And even if Isaiah never comes around, you have the rest of the community that will support you. Try to draw comfort from that."

"*Danke, meine schweschder.*" Adele placed her hands in Olivia's and drew strength. Come what may, *Gott* was with her, and Olivia was with her too. She needed to count her blessings, not tally her struggles.

Isaiah barely slept that night. He felt stunned—absolutely stupefied—by Adele's confession. It was the last thing he'd expected.

Rather than hoping to court a beautiful but shy woman, instead he learned she was a woman with a tremendous amount of baggage, not least of which was a baby being raised by her sister. It was a messy situation, far messier than he could possibly have imagined.

He wasn't sure he was capable of handling that baggage. He was a simple man, with simple hopes and dreams.

While he was initially drawn to Adele for the very thing that apparently had sent her spiraling into an abyss—her beauty—he was interested in courting her for the qualities that seemed to embody most Amish women: modesty, humility, a work ethic and genuine devoutness.

Plus, she was clearly fond of Phoebe, and his daughter was just as fond of Adele. That kind of warm relationship was critical if he should ever remarry. After that misunderstanding over the photo album, he now understood Adele had been trying everything in her power to sway Phoebe to stay in the church. But how could he accept as a wife someone with Adele's history?

He rose early and splashed his face with cold water. He hadn't heard a peep from Phoebe since she'd fled into her bedroom, and he was worried about the effects of Adele's confession on the teen. Youngies tended to internalize a lot and dramatize everything. Yet it would be hard to argue that Adele's confession wasn't horrifically dramatic, and he worried how Phoebe would respond.

He lit a fire in the wood cookstove and started the house warming. Since both he and Phoebe had missed dinner last night, he made a hearty breakfast of sausage, eggs and biscuits. While the food cooked, he dashed out to the barn to release the chickens and make sure their food and water was abundant. When he returned to the kitchen, he still saw no signs of his daughter.

When breakfast was ready, he knocked on her door. "Phoebe? *Leibling*, I've made breakfast. Are you hungry?"

He heard noises from within. "*Ja*," she said in a muffled voice. "I'll be right out."

Well, at least they were on speaking terms. Isaiah considered that a good sign.

It took ten minutes for her to emerge. She was dressed properly, but her eyes were red and swollen from crying.

"Ach, *liebling...*" Isaiah walked over and enveloped her in a huge bear hug.

"*Daed...*" Leaning into him, she started crying again.

He let her weep for a few minutes, then fished a clean handkerchief from his pocket. "Mop your face," he instructed gently.

She nodded and buried her face in the cloth, then blew her nose.

"*Komm* and eat breakfast," he said, guiding her toward the kitchen table. "Neither of us had anything to eat last night. We'll do better with something inside us."

Phoebe pulled out a chair and slumped down while Isaiah brought the hot food from the pans on the stovetop, including the biscuits that had been staying warm in the warming oven. From force of habit, he saw Phoebe close her eyes in a silent prayer, then she reached for some sausages.

Both were quiet for a few minutes until the pangs of hunger were gone. Isaiah poured her some tea, prepared the way he knew she liked it.

Finally Phoebe leaned back in her chair. "*Danke, Daed.* I was hungry."

"So was I." He eyed her. "Feeling better?"

"A bit." She toyed with the handle of her mug. "*Daed...* I may have been wrong about not getting baptized."

Isaiah's heart gave a great leap, but he kept his face entirely impassive. It was clear Phoebe had spent a lot of time thinking—and crying—and he wanted to encourage her to say what was on her mind.

"Is it because of Adele?" he asked gently.

"*Ja.*" She kept her eyes on her hot tea. "You know I've always wanted to travel, but I guess I'm old enough to think practically. How would I make a living in the *Englisch* world? Not from making carpets, of that I'm sure. I might be able to afford an apartment, but I wouldn't be able to afford much else. Certainly I couldn't afford to fly all around the world and live in fancy places. If someone as beautiful as Adele had to resort to…to low measures to enjoy the exotic lifestyle she did, how would I fare? I'm nowhere near as pretty. M-maybe I should set my sights closer to home."

Danke, Gott, Isaiah thought silently. If Adele had done nothing else, apparently she had been able to accomplish what he, Phoebe's own father, had been unable to.

"Don't give up hope of traveling, *liebling*," he told her. "People in the church travel all the time. But it should be a special thing once in a while, not a lifestyle."

"*Ja*, I realize that now. But something Adele said last night stuck with me. She said I have no idea how much support I'd be giving up if I left the church. She's right. I tried to think through—really think through—what I would do if I didn't have you and everyone else at my back. And… and I didn't like what I saw."

Isaiah was rocked by how mature his daughter suddenly sounded. It was like she had grown from a girl to a woman overnight.

"That's why *meidung*—shunning—is so painful," he said. "Not that you would be shunned if you refused to be baptized, but to give up the community that comes with being in the church is a huge step."

"*Ja*, I think I see that now." She looked up at him, and he saw fresh tears well in her eyes. "It's kind of strange, to give up what had been a dream of mine. I don't have anything yet that will take its place. I feel…empty inside. Or maybe I'm just cried out, I don't know."

His heart bled a little bit. Standing in as both mother and

father since his wife died, he now wished for a woman's instinctive wisdom to offer his daughter comfort.

As if snatching the thought from the air, Phoebe asked tentatively, "*Daed*? Are…are you still planning to court Adele?"

He knew the youngie would pose the question sooner or later, but he didn't have an answer. "I don't know, *liebling*," he said slowly. "I won't pretend hearing about her past wasn't a big blow. I'm still not sure how I feel about it. Like you, there's an emptiness inside me, and I don't know what will fill it." He paused a moment. "Knowing what you know now, how do you feel about her? You said earlier you wouldn't mind having her as a mother. Has that changed?"

"*N-nein*, I don't think so. I don't know… I'm confused too." Her head drooped.

A thought occurred to him, something that made him feel better. "I think I'm going to go talk to the bishop," he said. "He knows about Adele's past, but of course he wasn't about to discuss it with me. He might be able to offer me some guidance now that I know everything."

"When will you do that?"

"Probably this afternoon. I don't want to bother him too early in the day. I don't know if he has any appointments or commitments, but since tomorrow is an off-Sunday, he won't be preparing for a church service. Do you want to go?"

"*Nein*. I—I think I'll put up some Christmas decorations. There are some cedars near the barn. I can cut some branches and drape them across the window. Maybe I'll even make a wreath."

"*Gut* idea." He was heartened by her plan. Every year, she enjoyed decorating for Christmas. That it occurred to her now was a *gut* sign. He scraped back his chair. "*Komm*, let's tidy the kitchen. And I think," he added with a touch of levity, "I might be up for a nap later on. I barely slept last night."

"*Ja*, I'm still tired myself." She stood up and picked up her plate and cutlery.

Together they washed the dishes and wiped the counters.

"One thing is for certain," Phoebe ventured after a few minutes, as she dried a plate and reached into a cupboard to put it away. "Christmas will be a bit different than I thought. I—I have to admit, I was hoping to invite Adele over for Christmas dinner."

He was startled, since he'd never mentioned the possibility to her. "*Ja*, I confess I was thinking the same thing." He ruffled the top of her head just in front of her *kapp*, as he used to when she was younger. "We'll still have a fun Christmas, *liebling*. I know we're far away from our friends and relatives, but maybe we can have some of your new friends over on Christmas Day."

"*Ja gut*." She finished wiping down the counters and dried her hands on a dishtowel. "I'll go get a basket out of the barn, and I know where the nippers are."

"And I've got some chores to do before I go talk to the bishop."

He watched as she threw a cloak over her shoulders and made her way toward the barn. He was cautiously optimistic about Phoebe's change of heart…even though it came at a high cost.

He sighed and wondered what he could anticipate from the bishop. At this point, he was perfectly willing to put his future in *Gott*'s hands.

Chapter Fifteen

Adele returned to her cabin after visiting Olivia and Andrew. She'd tried to put baby Helen down for a nap, but without much success. The baby was bonded to her sister, not her. She was in a depressed frame of mind as she trudged up to the cabin and opened the door.

The kittens came tumbling over to greet her. Adele scooped them up and held them to her cheeks for a few moments. Olivia had a *hutband* and a baby to love her. While she had only…

She gently placed the kittens back on the floor and tossed a crumpled-up ball of paper for them to scamper after, then re-stoked the fire and put on a kettle for tea.

Slumped at the kitchen table, waiting for the kettle to boil, she dozed, exhausted from the emotional turmoil and sleepless night.

A knock on the door startled her awake. For a wild moment her heart hoped it was Isaiah before her mind denied it. Knuckling weariness from her eyes, she stumbled for the door and opened it.

Phoebe stood on the porch, holding a wreath made of cedar branches. Adele barely saw the item. She only had eyes for the youngie to whom she had hoped she might someday become a stepmother.

Phoebe spoke first. "Are you okay?"

"I should ask the same question about you," Adele replied. "Aw, *komm* here..."

She opened her arms, and the teen dropped the wreath and pitched into them. Adele felt the girl's shoulders heave. Her own eyes stung.

When she pulled back, Phoebe's mouth was contorted in an effort not to cry. "Can you come inside?" asked Adele. "I was just making some tea."

"*Ja*. I think *Daed*'s restriction on seeing you is probably lifted at this point, although...well, he's not home, so he doesn't know I'm here."

"*Liebling*, I don't want to get you into any more trouble," warned Adele.

"I'm already in trouble. What's a little more?" Phoebe reached down to pick up the wreath. "Here. I made this for you."

"For me?" Adele spread a hand across her chest. "It's beautiful! I didn't know you had such talent."

"I started decorating the house today and made one for our own front door. I thought you might like one too."

Adele wanted to weep all over again. She felt she hardly deserved the youngie's charitable kindness. "I will hang it up this evening. Gracious, it smells so *gut*." She breathed deeply of the forest scent.

Phoebe stooped to pet the kittens that came tumbling up then hoisted both animals in her arms to cuddle them. "I love these little things."

"*Ja*, they're *gut* company." Adele pulled out the tea things and put the steaming kettle on the edge of the stove. "Sit down, child, and choose which kind of tea you'd like."

Phoebe released the animals and chose a tea bag, then

plopped down onto one of the kitchen chairs. "I came over to tell you something."

"*Ja*?" Adele poured hot water into two mugs.

"I think I've changed my mind about being baptized."

Adele paused in her task and met the girl's eyes. Maybe it was her imagination, but there seemed to be a sort of bitter peace in them. "Is it because of me?" she asked quietly.

"*Ja.*" Phoebe took a deep and shuddering breath. "I didn't sleep well last night. I kept thinking about all those places you saw, then started wondering how I could afford to see them. I told *Daed* this morning that I never really stopped to consider the reality of what it would be like to be utterly without the support of my family or the wider church. I'd probably be working a minimum-wage job, and while I might be able to support myself, I certainly couldn't go traveling all over the world."

Adele closed her eyes. *Danke, Gott*, she thought. Then she opened her eyes and focused on the tea bag she was dipping up and down in the hot water of her mug. "How did your father take it?"

"He didn't do any backflips, you understand, but I know he was relieved. He told me I could still travel, but it would have to be something special I'd save up for, rather than a lifestyle."

"*Liebling*, speaking as someone who did everything backward, I have to admit the wisdom of that. I would have enjoyed seeing New Zealand or Paris if it was a once-every-few-years treat, rather than jet-setting from one to the other without pause. I wouldn't have looked back at everything with shame too."

"I guess now I have to think differently about my future," said Phoebe thoughtfully. "It's like there's a big hole inside me that used to be filled with dreams of seeing the world. Now I have to fill up that hole."

"Now here's another question," Adele asked with a smile. "Was it a burning interest in travel that captured you, or did you just want to escape the church?"

"Maybe a little of both," the teen confessed. "I was fighting and fighting against it, but ignoring all the benefits it gives me. Now that I think about it, that's not a logical way to look at things."

"But that's not unusual among youngies," said Adele. She gave the girl a rueful grin. "Ask me how I know."

"And you gave it all up to come back to the church."

"*Ja.* I mean, look at my sister, Olivia, and her *hutband*, Andrew. They did everything right, and as a result they have great peace of mind and no regrets. I didn't realize until recently how valuable those assets were. I can always look at pictures of faraway places and dream of visiting them, and none of that will have a bad impact on my life. But because I wasn't satisfied with just *looking* at pictures, I have many regrets and didn't acquire peace of mind until I stopped what I was doing. Does that make sense?"

"*Ja*, I suppose..." Phoebe's voice trailed off.

"*Liebling.*" Adele wrapped her hands around the warmth of the mug. "Nothing says you have to be baptized tomorrow. Seventeen is a bit too young anyway.

Now is your chance to flounder around and try to find some work that you can enjoy doing. Your rugs are beautiful, and you could probably sell them nationwide, if you were inclined. But you're such a talented youngie, you could put your hands or mind to almost anything. Just don't forget the support you're getting from the church, and think long and hard before you give that up."

"I see that now." A rare smile lit up the girl's face, making her look very pretty, despite the dark circles under her eyes. "I think I can promise you this, I won't look too far away. I've made some friends about my age here, and they're just finishing their *Rumspringa* too. I know the *Englisch* friends I had back in Indiana made *Daed* worried, but these new friends aren't interested in leaving the church, so I suppose *Daed* can stop worrying."

"I don't think that's possible," Adele replied ruefully. "I think parents always worry about their *kinner*, no matter what age. Does it bother you?"

"*Ja*, sometimes." Phoebe picked at the edge of her mug. "I mean, I know he wants what's right for me, and I also know he feels bad that my *mamm* died when I was such a young age, and I have no woman to look up to. Except you," she added.

Adele groaned. "I'm about the last woman you should look up to, *liebling*."

"But I do," said Phoebe seriously. "And I don't just mean because you traveled everywhere or had a bad life. I mean because you're living a *gut* life now. You left it all behind. That's important."

The praise was not only unexpected, but also a startlingly mature observation for someone so young. It warmed Adele to the soles of her feet. "*Danke, liebling*," she said softly.

Phoebe swallowed the last of her tea. "I should get going," she said. "I don't want *Daed* to catch me not at home. I—I still have your photo album," she added awkwardly. "What should I do with it?"

Adele suppressed the advice to burn it. It wasn't Phoebe's job to take that kind of a drastic step. "Just hang on to it," she said. "I'm sure you'll have the chance to return it at some point. I'm just embarrassed you saw some of those photos."

"I'm really sorry I took it," the teen said glumly.

"In a way, maybe it worked out for the best," Adele said more heartily than she felt. "It changed a lot of things for both of us. For all three of us, including your *daed*."

"Now we'll see what comes of it." Phoebe stood up, gave Adele a fierce hug and disappeared out the door.

Adele watched the teen until she disappeared from sight. Then she picked up the lovely cedar wreath and thought about where to hang it.

Isaiah didn't quite know what to expect from his visit with the bishop. Was he seeking advice? Counseling? A sympathetic ear? He didn't know. He just hoped for clarity of some sort.

He approached the bishop's house, a made-over barn perched on a wide lawn amidst the pines and firs. Smoke rose from the stove pipe, indicating the couple was home.

He climbed the porch steps and knocked. After a moment, the door whisked open to reveal Lois, the bishop's wife. She had a smudge of flour on her apron. She looked surprised to see him. "*Guten tag*, Isaiah!"

"*Guten tag*. I'm sorry to drop in unannounced. Is your *hutband* at home?"

"*Ja*, he's in his office. *Komm* in." She stepped aside.

Isaiah entered the house, redolent with delicious smells. He unbuttoned his coat and hung it on a coat rack near the door, followed by his black felt hat.

"I'm just doing some Christmas baking," Lois explained. "Would you like to bring some cookies home for you and Phoebe?"

"*Ja*, *danke*," he replied politely, his mind far away from cookies. "Phoebe would like that, I'm sure."

"Let me go get Samuel." She disappeared into another part of the house.

She reemerged in a moment with the church leader in her wake. "*Guten tag*, Isaiah," he said. "Is something wrong?"

"*Ja*. I'm hoping you can advise me, if you have some time to spare."

"I'll just keep working in the kitchen," said Lois diplomatically, and turned to leave.

"Actually, Lois, your input might be valuable," said Isaiah.

"*Ja gut*. Then why don't you both come into the kitchen? I have things in the oven I don't want to ignore."

Isaiah allowed himself to be seated at the kitchen table. The room was chaotic with baking in all stages—platters of frosted and decorated cookies at one end and raw dough at the other. Without asking, Lois poured coffee and set cups at both his and her husband's elbows before picking up a rolling pin and flattening some dough. She said nothing, but Isaiah could almost see her ears prick under her *kapp*.

"It's about Adele," he began. "Well, Adele and Phoebe."

He went through the events of last night and touched on the contents of the photo album without getting too graphic. He explained how Phoebe told him she wasn't sure about getting baptized, and—after finding the album—about his erroneous conclusion that Adele was trying to influence his daughter away from the church.

"I'm not proud of how I confronted her on her doorstep," he admitted. "I was wrong to accuse her of that. But then she came over afterward and demanded I listen to her. She admitted everything."

"Everything?" clarified the bishop. "What do you mean, *everything*?"

"Probably everything you already know," he said with a rueful and humorless smile. "Everything you danced around as being told to you in confidence, I suspect I now know. Certainly she confessed what kind of lifestyle she led over the past fifteen years."

The bishop's nostrils flared as he leaned back in his chair and steepled his fingers. "That must have taken a lot of courage," he said cautiously.

Had it? That was one thing Isaiah hadn't really factored in—how much bravery it took to own up to such a past. "I guess it explains why she spent the past two months barely speaking to me, despite the fact that we work together," he replied. "I also understand better why both you and her sister recommended she steer clear of men."

"*Ja*," the church leader admitted. "I felt it would be best if she focused on forging new behaviors that didn't involve her...her previous habits."

"And it's those 'previous habits' that have me worried," admitted Isaiah. "Finding out almost destroyed Phoebe. She spent the whole night crying, as far as I can tell. This morning she told me she was reconsidering her reluctance to get baptized. So if nothing else, I guess Adele helped with that."

"But where does that leave you?" inquired Lois. She pressed cookie cutters into the dough, forming shapes of pine trees and candy canes. "You said you were thinking about courting her. Does her past change that?"

"*Ja*," said Isaiah slowly, his eyes on Lois's handiwork. "It's...it's a huge hurdle, I confess. I don't know if I can overlook it. It would be one thing if her...indiscretions were a one-time thing, but she admits she made a life of it—for fifteen years, no less. I thought she was just an unusually shy and modest woman who might have suffered some sort of abuse in her past. Now I learn she was..."

"Isaiah." The bishop crossed his arms on his chest and regarded him sternly. "One of the most famous stories in the Bible involves a Samaritan woman at the well whose past was every bit as colorful as Adele's. What was the lesson in that story?"

"Forgiveness," muttered Isaiah.

"*Ja.* And there's another famous story of a woman brought up on charges of adultery. What was the lesson in that story?"

"That sinners shouldn't cast stones." Isaiah felt like a child being lectured, and wasn't sure he liked it.

"*Ja.* And what was the adulterous woman told after all her accusers left?"

Isaiah groped, trying to remember the exact phrase, but the words escaped him.

Into the silence, Lois said softly, "Go and sin no more."

"*Ja*, right," replied the bishop. "Adele has left behind her sinful life. What she is doing is not easy. She's watching her own sister raise the baby she abandoned, yet she's willing to deal with the stone-throwers because she wants so badly to be redeemed. Will you deny her that opportunity?"

"Of course not," Isaiah replied crossly. "But that doesn't mean I should be the one responsible for that redemption." The moment the words escaped his lips, he felt ashamed. He had just thrown stones. Big ones.

Sure enough, the bishop's eyes cooled. "You're the one asking for clarity on your feelings for Adele now that you know about her past. Your feelings are your own, and they're between you and *Gott.* You're certainly under no obligation to court Adele or any other woman. What I'm saying is that if you *do* choose to court her, you must never—under any circumstances—hold her past over her head, especially since she is so desperate to leave it behind. Instead, you must help her heal and move forward. Unless and until you can do this, you should not court her."

"I see." What else had he expected? Some magical way he could alter his emotions about Adele? Like the scribes and Pharisees who had dragged in the adulterous woman for tribunal, he felt like slinking away in shame.

Lois pulled some freshly baked cookies out of the oven and placed the hot cookie sheets on cooling racks. "How is Phoebe doing?" she asked. "Have her feelings for Adele changed?"

"There were some awkward moments when Adele had to explain the reality of her previous life," Isaiah said dryly. "It was shocking for Phoebe, to say the least. But the reason Adele got into details in the first place was because she told Phoebe she was trying to save her from a lifetime of regret. I think that's what bothered Phoebe most of all—that her idol was suddenly so flawed. But I know she's very fond of Adele. Fond enough that when I mentioned the possibility of courting her a day ago, Phoebe lit up with smiles and said she'd love to have Adele as a mother." Isaiah slumped over his coffee cup. "But how can I provide her with a mother like that?"

"There's no easy answer," said Lois, using a spatula to lift the cooling cookies. "But perhaps having a sadder-but-wiser woman standing in as a mother figure is just what an impressionable youngie needs to stay on the straight and narrow. Whenever Phoebe starts to get restless and look at the wider world, Adele can remind her to look at the bigger picture, not just the exotic snippets."

"And remember," warned the bishop, "nothing has to be decided right now. Adele is a long way from being baptized. For that matter, so is Phoebe, since she's only seventeen and has at least a year, if not more, before I'll consider her for baptism. That's a lot of time for all parties to think things through. I can tell you this, though—I feel very protective of Adele, and I'm also deeply impressed with her. It's not everyone who can recognize a sinful path and change their ways so utterly and completely. I'm pleased with her progress and respect her as a redeemed woman."

Respect her as a redeemed woman. Isaiah almost winced, since the bishop beat him out for charity when it came to considering Adele's past.

"I guess I haven't yet gotten to that point," he admitted, feeling shame for his inability.

"Well, the news is fresh," conceded the bishop. "I've known about the situation for months. You just found out. Plus your interest in Adele is different than mine. I see her as part of the church family. You were thinking of her as a future wife and mother for your daughter. That's a massively different dynamic."

"Then I guess I have some thinking to do." Isaiah pushed his untouched cup of coffee aside and rose. "*Vielen dank* for hearing me out."

Lois took a small cardboard box, lined it with a clean dishcloth and piled it high with decorated Christmas cookies. "For you and Phoebe," she said, handing him the gift.

The simple gesture made Isaiah blink hard. "*Vielen dank*," he repeated.

Moments later, he had donned his coat and hat and was walking down the road toward home, the box tucked under his arm.

There were more than enough cookies for himself and Phoebe. In fact, there were enough cookies to share. Isaiah wondered if that was Lois's intent.

Chapter Sixteen

Isaiah walked up the driveway to his new farm, the box of cookies securely under his arm. He paused for a moment and looked at the bushes and vegetation that blocked the view of the rental cabin next door. A few minutes more, and he could be on Adele's doorstep, apologizing. He owed her that much, at least, for accusing her of leading his daughter away from the church.

But he didn't. Instead, he turned down his driveway and headed up the porch steps to his own house.

He paused and admired the cedar wreath Phoebe had made. His daughter loved decorating the house for Christmas, and he was pleased to be able to offer her some of Lois Beiler's Christmas cookies.

"I'm back," he announced unnecessarily, opening the door. The house smelled fragrant with pine boughs.

Phoebe looked up from another wreath she was making, then back down at her work. "How went the meeting with the bishop?" she asked, her voice a bit muffled.

"Fine. Lois Beiler gave me these to take home." He placed the box of cookies on the table.

"Yum!" Phoebe dove for one of the colorful creations and took a bite. "Your meeting was just 'fine'? What did he say about Adele?"

Isaiah wasn't sure he was ready to discuss with his teenage daughter all the intricacies of his conversation. "Not a lot I'm willing to tell," he said, tempering his words with a smile. "But let's just say I have a lot to think about."

"Oh." Phoebe laid the half-eaten cookie down beside her and continued weaving cedar branches with colorful ribbons. "*Daed*… I've been thinking. Maybe I should go talk to the bishop too. I know I'm too young to start taking classes toward baptism, but it wouldn't hurt to talk with him about…well, about my future."

Isaiah dropped into the kitchen chair opposite his daughter and reached for a cookie. "Are you serious about this?" he asked gently. "I'm trying not to stand up and cheer, you understand, but I also know this has to be your decision."

"Yet you were willing to forbid me from seeing Adele because you thought she was a bad influence," Phoebe replied with some asperity.

Isaiah couldn't deny the truth. "*Ja*, you're right. And I was wrong to do that on two counts. One, I was just plain wrong when I thought she was a bad influence. And two, Adele herself told me the harder I try to make you stay in the church, the more you're likely to pull away. *Liebling*, while it's painful to think you may not want to stay, I know as a father I have to let you make your own decision."

His daughter was silent a few moments, her hands busy with the wreath. "I went to see Adele this afternoon while you were away," she confessed. "We had a *gut* talk. I didn't realize how much support I would lose if I left the church, and what Adele told us last night reinforces that. She asked if I really wanted to travel, or if I just wanted to get away and do my own thing. I said maybe a little of both."

"I think," Isaiah said thoughtfully, "Adele is a wiser woman than I realized, even though I've been working with her for a while." He felt moved to more compassion now that Adele seemed instrumental in setting his daughter closer to the straight and narrow path.

"Are you still going to court her?" asked Phoebe hesitantly.

"Do you think I should?"

"Well… I like her. I like her a lot." With a hint of pertness, she added, "You could do worse."

Isaiah laughed. That sounded like his old Phoebe, full of sass. "Lois Beiler gave me more cookies than either you or I can eat," he said. "Maybe I should bring some to Adele."

"*Ja*, maybe you should," his daughter replied with a smile. "And maybe you should do it *right now*. And here…" She got up and jogged into her bedroom, then emerged a moment later with the infamous photo album. "Give this back to her."

Adele sat quietly in the rocking chair she had pulled closer to the woodstove. The temperature outside was dipping near freezing, though there was no snow on the ground yet, and the warmth of the stove felt good. Pale afternoon sunlight streamed through the windows.

She had finished embroidering one of the two ornaments she had planned to make. Phoebe's had turned out lovely, and she hoped the youngie would like it.

She was a little more uncertain whether she would be giving Isaiah his ornament or not. Perhaps he might not welcome such a gift, in which case she could keep it herself, and maybe hang it from the lovely wreath Phoebe had given her.

She stitched and thought and thought and stitched. Despite Phoebe's visit that morning, Adele didn't have a lot of hope Isaiah would come around. While she was certain he would forgive her for the misunderstanding about Phoebe's possession of the photo album, she was equally certain he wouldn't be interested in courting a fallen woman. She mentally braced herself for his subtle scorn and cooled-off interest at work on Monday.

And in a way, she was okay with it. Isaiah had never been part of her long-term plan to become baptized anyway. Her future was likely to remain here, living in a rental cabin, giving affection to her two kittens and playing the part of aunt to her own daughter as the child grew up with Olivia and Andrew.

However narrow that future seemed, it was at least respectable. At this point, Adele's desperation to remain respectable outdid all other criteria, including romance.

She heard a knock at the door. Her hands froze in the act of taking a stitch, while her heart began to pound. It wasn't likely to be Phoebe. Nor was it likely to be Olivia. That left only…

She rose to her feet and hastily stuffed the half-finished ornament in a kitchen drawer. She smoothed down her apron, patted her *kapp* to make sure it was properly in place, then padded to the front door and opened it.

Isaiah stood on the porch, his expression sober, a shoebox-size cardboard box clutched in one hand and her photo album in the other. "*Guten tag*, Adele," he said quietly. "May I come in?"

"*Ja* sure." She could hardly refuse.

He entered the room. The kittens lifted their heads and blinked at him sleepily from their basket near the woodstove.

"Here." A little awkwardly, he pushed the box toward her. The open top was covered by a white dishcloth. "Lois

Beiler sent me home with these, and there were too many for just Phoebe and me."

She took the box and peeked under the cloth to find a dozen colorfully decorated Christmas cookies. "*Danke*," she said, not quite sure what to make of the peace offering. If Lois Beiler had given him the fresh cookies, it was proof he had been to see the bishop.

"And I brought this back too," he added. "Phoebe wanted to make sure I gave it back to you."

The last thing Adele wanted to see was that cursed photo album, but better to have it in her hands than in Isaiah's—or Phoebe's. "*Danke*," she said again. She took the album and slipped it onto a bookshelf.

"We need to talk," he continued. "Is this a *gut* time?"

"As *gut* a time as any." She suppressed the leap of hope his words gave her. If he was willing to talk, maybe he was willing to do more. "Do you want some tea?"

"*Ja* sure." He shrugged out of his coat and hung it on a hook by the door, followed by his black felt hat.

Glad to have something to do with her hands, she placed the box of cookies on the kitchen table, sweeping aside the embroidery debris. He sat down and watched as she awkwardly went about filling the kettle, placing it on the stove and gathering tea things.

"Phoebe told me she came to see you earlier today," he said after a while.

"*Ja*," she replied. "And she told me you had gone to talk to the bishop." She met his eyes gravely. "I won't ask what you discussed."

"You can ask all you want, since you were the subject of the discussion." Isaiah closed his eyes and pinched the bridge of his nose. "Look, Adele, I won't pretend your background didn't come as a shock to me. To be honest, it was the last thing I expected. I wasn't sure how I should feel about it. I suspect you know I was thinking about courting you, but now..."

Adele's heart sank, but she kept her face impassive. It was just as she'd thought. All the self-loathing she had worked so hard to conquer welled up and threatened to consume her.

"I hope you know I went to the bishop months ago and made a full confession," she said wearily. "He knows everything. I made sure there were no secrets about what I'd done that might derail my goal of joining the church."

"I know that now. Samuel Beiler gave me a *gut* lecture on the Samaritan woman at the well and the woman who was going to be stoned for adultery. No offense, of course, but the parallels are clear."

"Of course." The stories of those two biblical women were very familiar to Adele.

"I felt like a youngie back at school being scolded by a teacher," he admitted with a grimace. "Samuel made sure I extracted the obvious lessons from both accounts. He also made sure I understood I shouldn't disregard those lessons when dealing with you, the lessons of forgiveness and throwing stones..."

His voice trailed off. Adele stiffened her spine and sat down on the kitchen chair opposite him. "Isaiah, you need to understand something about how I grew up before you start to question why I made the bad choices I did. It has everything to do with being beautiful. It's a curse."

She saw his eyes widen. "How can beauty be a curse?"

"Because sometimes it can supersede character development. You've seen my sister, Olivia. She's plain as an iron bucket. When we were younger, that caused some resentment, as you can imagine, but she has great strength of character and learned to cultivate her skills and personality. Now look at her—she's happily married to a *gut* man and is the most sensible person I know. But for myself...well, I learned early on that my looks were a weapon I could wield like a sword. As long as I made the right moves, men would fall at my feet and do anything I asked. That's a powerful and dangerously seductive tool for a youngie, and it skewed my thinking and my behavior for many years."

"In what way?" His voice was quiet.

"In the way of never developing any inner strength. I didn't have to—my face was the key to everything. Olivia has strength in abundance. I have nothing. I never needed it...until recently. But it's a sad thing to have no self-confidence. Olivia pointed out that I never learned to love myself, since I always depended on my beauty to get by. When she said that, it was like a key turned in a lock. It made so much sense. I was always afraid to stand on my own two feet. It was far easier to let a man prop me up."

The kettle on the stove started whistling, so Adele got up and poured the hot water into mugs. Isaiah was silent for a few moments as he dipped a tea bag up and down. "I won't deny that's what first attracted me," he admitted. "Any man would notice how beautiful you are."

His words confirmed the disillusionment within Adele. "*Ja*, I know." She heard the cynicism in her own voice. "It's been that way since I was Phoebe's age or even younger. Until I came here, I cultivated that to the nth degree. I made a career out of it."

He winced. Then he said something unexpected. "Tell me about your baby."

Adele was startled. The memory of how she'd handled Helen's infancy brought pain. She sighed. "I named her after my mother, who died when I was five years old," she said. "I didn't know until later that she was born on the very day my *daed* died. Olivia had spent a long time caring for him during his final illness. He'd always wanted grandchildren, but I'd left the church and Olivia wasn't married, so he never got his wish—that he knew of. He died without knowing I was to be redeemed. It's a regret I'll carry to my grave."

"You didn't stay in contact with him?"

"Not very often. I'd dip back into Olivia's life every so often, usually between men and when my finances were tight, but I was too ashamed to talk much with my *daed*. He never reproved me or was angry with me, but he was incredibly sad about the path I took, so it was easier to avoid him. The last time I saw him was about four years ago. I didn't even know he was ill."

She closed her eyes against the pain and spent a moment mastering her emotions.

"Abandoning Helen was probably the lowest point of my life, but I knew I couldn't live the lifestyle I had been living with an infant in tow. And I didn't know what else to do to survive except…except to continue doing what I was doing. Olivia's always been my rock, and I knew she would take the baby."

"You traveled all the way to rural Montana just to abandon her?" asked Isaiah.

"*Ja*. And that underscores how much of a sinner I am."

"Will it be difficult to live in the same community as your sister, knowing she's raising your child? What will Helen think when she gets older?"

Adele got a glimpse of where Isaiah was going with this. "Olivia made it clear she won't give Helen up," she said. "And I don't want her to. She and Andrew have adopted her as their own. Too many people know the truth of her parentage, so it won't be a secret. Olivia and I have derived an explanation for when Helen is old enough to understand: That Aunt Adele wasn't able to take care of her when she was born, so *Mamm* and *Daed* stepped in to take care of her, etcetera. My prayer is that she doesn't grow up rebellious like I was, especially since she shows every promise of inheriting my looks."

"I see." He sipped his tea. "I guess I'm just trying to gauge what impact she may have on our…on *your* life in the future."

At his slip of the tongue, Adele looked at him sharply. "Why do you care?" she asked.

He paused for a moment then said slowly, "Because I can't get it out of my head that *Gott* wants me to court you."

She bit her lip. "Isaiah, I have so much baggage… I don't know if I'm the right person to become your wife."

"And yet, as I said, I can't shake the prospect."

"Are you sure it's not just because I'm beautiful?"

"That's only part of the whole. But my biggest concern is Phoebe, of course. She's been my world since my late wife passed away, especially since we couldn't have any other *kinner*. Phoebe is so fond of you…"

"As I am of her. But that doesn't mean you have to marry me. Phoebe and I can be *gut* friends without getting you involved."

"Would you *want* me to court you?" Isaiah asked. She heard a trace of uncertainty in his voice.

Would she? Marriage meant permanence. She had never had that in her life. Men came and went, and she didn't dare risk falling in love, because she knew the relationship wouldn't last. She was attracted to Isaiah, but she was scared to death to admit she loved him. Scared to death.

So she told him that. "While, in theory, getting married

sounds like the right thing to do, I don't know how *gut* a wife I would be," she concluded and fought back tears. "You're too fine a man to be saddled with a fallen woman who doesn't have the slightest clue how to be a wife."

Oddly, her words seemed to clear away the uncertainty in his expression. "That's one of the things the bishop told me," he said with a small smile. "He said if I choose to court you, I must never, under any circumstances, hold your past over your head. Samuel admires you a lot," he added. "He says he's pleased with your progress and respects you as a redeemed woman."

"Does he?" Adele was surprised and touched at the church leader's regard. "I didn't know that."

"So if you feel uncertain, we can take it slow. You're not baptized yet anyway, and won't be for another year or so." He held out his hands on the table, palms up. "But, Adele—I'd like to court you."

After a moment's hesitation, she laid her hands in his and felt his fingers tighten around hers. Her eyes prickled again. "Are you sure, Isaiah? There are any number of women, young widows perhaps, you could court."

"But they're not *you*. Adele, if you're concerned you're not *gut* enough for me, put it aside. But if you decide in the end you'd rather not marry me, I'll understand and not hold anything against you. We've only known each other a short amount of time. The next year will be a time of tremendous change for you, hopefully for the better, and hopefully in my favor." He gave her a slow smile.

Could she do it? She didn't know, but she kept her fingers laced with his. "How does Phoebe feel about the possibility of courtship?"

"Over the moon."

That brought a smile to her face. "I hope Helen turns out

to be half as fine a daughter as Phoebe." A thought occurred to her, hitting her with abrupt urgency. She withdrew her hands from his. "Hang on, there's something I need to do."

She walked over and fetched the infamous photo album off the bookshelf. It was in binder form, and she snapped open the three rings. Without a word, she withdrew one page, covered back and front with photos. She opened the door of the woodstove and put it in.

"Are you sure, Adele?" asked Isaiah as the flames caught the page and began burning it.

"*Ja*," she replied. She withdrew a second page and fed it to the flames. "I'm a different person than I was a year ago. Even three months ago. I don't want anything to remind me of my former life." She fed a third page to the flames.

Isaiah was silent as she methodically withdrew each page, perhaps thirty total, and inserted them into the woodstove. When she was finished, she snapped the rings closed and pushed the empty binder toward him. "Need a binder?"

He laughed. "*Nein*. Feel better?"

"Actually, *ja*." She rewarded him with a bright smile. "I feel lighter somehow. That's something I should have done a long time ago." She sat down at the table and picked up her mug of tea.

"That took some courage." The look on his face was one of admiration. "You know what, Adele? I think I just fell in love."

Her heart flopped over. Her voice trembled. "Is this c-courtship?"

"*Ja*. I think it is." He held out his hands again.

Epilogue

Adele's eyes sparkled with pleasure as she listened to the ancient words intoned by the bishop during the baptismal ceremony. "Are you willing, by the help and grace of God, to renounce the world, the devil, your own flesh and blood, and be obedient only to God and His church?"

The response was firm. "*Ja.*"

The ceremony continued, then concluded with water pouring from the bishop's cupped hands over her bowed head. "I baptize you in the name of the Father…" More water. "And of the Son…" More water. "And of the Holy Spirit. *Amein.*"

Phoebe removed her hand from her face and smiled at the bishop, blinking through the drops running down her face. Lois Beiler handed her a clean handkerchief and waited until Phoebe mopped up, then—grinning—leaned down and kissed her cheek. "*Welkom,*" she murmured.

"*Danke.*" Smiling, the eighteen-year-old stood up, now a full-fledged member of the church, and placed her *kapp* back over her damp hair.

Isaiah stepped forward and hugged his daughter, and Adele saw him blinking back tears of joy.

Adele felt water trickle down her face, and for a moment thought they were her own tears. But no, it was just the remnants of the baptismal water the bishop had poured over her head a few minutes before.

Her heart swelled with gratitude and humility to be a full-fledged member of the church at last. It only took sixteen years, she reflected ruefully, but she knew by now *Gott* wouldn't hold that against her.

Nor would Isaiah. She could feel his eyes from across the barn where he had reseated himself on the men's side, and she blushed and ducked her head.

After the solemn ritual of baptism, the church service was by no means over; Adele knelt through a lengthy prayer, then listened to the benediction and sang the last hymn.

But after the congregants spilled outside into the bright late-October sunshine, Olivia surged up, eighteen-month-old Helen in her arms, and hugged Adele. "I'm so happy," she whispered.

"Not half as much as I am." Adele hugged her sister, then—as little Helen held out her arms toward her "aunt"—reached out to take the child.

She saw Phoebe, surrounded by an excited and chattering group of young people—and one *Englisch* young man, the same young man who had admired Phoebe at the house-raising the year before. While Adele didn't know much about Jeremy, she had a suspicion his interest in Phoebe was drawing him toward the Amish. It would be interesting to see how this played out over the next few years.

"One more month," murmured a voice in her ear.

She whirled, Helen still in her arms, and smiled at the man who would be her *hutband* within four weeks. "Just think," she told him. "A year from now, the *boppli* in my arms may be yours and mine."

"I don't care if *bopplin* come or not. That's up to *Gott*. I just care that you'll be my wife."

That was all Adele cared about too. Over the past year of courtship, Isaiah had proven himself to be everything she had come to admire in Amish men—steady and faithful and hardworking and loving.

And she—who had never been loved by a man, despite her past—still could not believe *Gott* had seen fit to send her a man like Isaiah.

"Prayers really do come true," she told him.

He sneaked a kiss. "*Ja*, they do," he murmured.

* * * * *

Dear Reader,

I've always maintained that the easiest way to a simpler life is to make good choices. But here's the thing: None of us walk on water, and often the choices we've made in our past are poor ones.

But while we cannot change our past, we can make better decisions in the future. This is the path my character Adele has taken as she strives to return to the church. It's my hope that her example will demonstrate the redeeming power of divine forgiveness.

I love hearing from readers and invite emails at patricelewis@protonmail.com.

Patrice Lewis

Get up to 4 Free Books!

We'll send you 2 free books from each series you try PLUS a free Mystery Gift.

Both the **Love Inspired®** and **Love Inspired® Suspense** series feature compelling novels filled with inspirational romance, faith, forgiveness and hope.

YES! Please send me 2 FREE novels from the Love Inspired or Love Inspired Suspense series and my FREE gift (gift is worth about $10 retail). After receiving them, if I don't wish to receive any more books, I can return the shipping statement marked "cancel." If I don't cancel, I will receive 6 brand-new Love Inspired Larger-Print books or Love Inspired Suspense Larger-Print books every month and be billed just $7.19 each in the U.S. or $7.99 each in Canada. That is a savings of 20% off the cover price. It's quite a bargain! Shipping and handling is just 50¢ per book in the U.S. and $1.25 per book in Canada.* I understand that accepting the 2 free books and gift places me under no obligation to buy anything. I can always return a shipment and cancel at any time by calling the number below. The free books and gift are mine to keep no matter what I decide.

Choose one: ☐ **Love Inspired Larger-Print** (122/322 BPA G36Y) ☐ **Love Inspired Suspense Larger-Print** (107/307 BPA G36Y) ☐ **Or Try Both!** (122/322 & 107/307 BPA G36Z)

Name (please print)

Address Apt. #

City State/Province Zip/Postal Code

Email: Please check this box ☐ if you would like to receive newsletters and promotional emails from Harlequin Enterprises ULC and its affiliates. You can unsubscribe anytime.

Mail to the **Harlequin Reader Service:**
IN U.S.A.: P.O. Box 1341, Buffalo, NY 14240-8531
IN CANADA: P.O. Box 603, Fort Erie, Ontario L2A 5X3

Want to explore our other series or interested in ebooks? Visit www.ReaderService.com or call 1-800-873-8635.

*Terms and prices subject to change without notice. Prices do not include sales taxes, which will be charged (if applicable) based on your state or country of residence. Canadian residents will be charged applicable taxes. Offer not valid in Quebec. This offer is limited to one order per household. Books received may not be as shown. Not valid for current subscribers to the Love Inspired or Love Inspired Suspense series. All orders subject to approval. Credit or debit balances in a customer's account(s) may be offset by any other outstanding balance owed by or to the customer. Please allow 4 to 6 weeks for delivery. Offer available while quantities last.

Your Privacy—Your information is being collected by Harlequin Enterprises ULC, operating as Harlequin Reader Service. For a complete summary of the information we collect, how we use this information and to whom it is disclosed, please visit our privacy notice located at https://corporate.harlequin.com/privacy-notice. Notice to California Residents – Under California law, you have specific rights to control and access your data. For more information on these rights and how to exercise them, visit https://corporate.harlequin.com/california-privacy. For additional information for residents of other U.S. states that provide their residents with certain rights with respect to personal data, visit https://corporate.harlequin.com/other-state-residents-privacy-rights/.

LIRLIS25